AF279286

*Jesus said to her, "Mary!" She turned
and said to Him in Hebrew, "Rabboni!"
(which means, Teacher). Jesus said to her,
"Stop clinging to Me, for I have not yet
ascended to the Father; but go to My
brothers and say to them, 'I am ascending
to My Father and your Father, and My
God and your God.'" Mary Magdalene
came and announced to the disciples,
"I have seen the Lord," and that He had
said these things to her.*

—John 20:16–18 (NASB)

Extraordinary Women of the BIBLE

HIGHLY FAVORED: MARY'S STORY
SINS AS SCARLET: RAHAB'S STORY
A HARVEST OF GRACE: RUTH AND NAOMI'S STORY
AT HIS FEET: MARY MAGDALENE'S STORY

AT HIS FEET

MARY MAGDALENE'S STORY

Roseanna M. White

AT HIS FEET

MARY MAGDALENE'S STORY

DEDICATION

To Kimberly and Martin, Aunt Mary Jane and Fred,
sponsors on a journey leading me ever onward
to worship at His feet

ACKNOWLEDGMENTS

Writing a book is always a joy (and hard work!), but this one was also an honor. I'm so grateful for the chance to be part of this series and to bring to life one of the most well-known but also mysterious women mentioned in the Bible. For my research, I turned primarily to a book called *Saint Mary Magdalene*, written by Fr. Sean Davidson, an Irish priest who spent decades serving in France. My gratitude goes out to Fr. Davidson for putting English words to the millennia-old French traditions that shed light on this beloved biblical figure.

I must also thank the amazing people who surround and encourage me—the brilliant team of editors at Guideposts; my seemingly-all-knowing agent, Steve; my best friend and critique partner, Stephanie; the supportive and encouraging ladies who make up my Patrons & Peers group, who cheered me through the writing of this one; my assistant, Rachel, without whom my online world would grind to a halt; my crazy-supportive husband, David, and kids, Xoë and Rowyn; my awesome parents and grandparents and sister; and all the readers who give me purpose.

Thank you all for helping me do this thing I love best and for equipping me to do it. I pray that, with this book, as with all my books, the Lord will take my efforts and use them for His glory.

CHAPTER ONE

FRIDAY

They had crowned the King with thorns.

Magdalene felt the pierce of each small sword in her heart as she watched the blood well up on the Master's brow and stream down His face. That precious, familiar face. How many times had she watched emotions move over each feature? She had seen Him laugh. She had seen Him frown. She had seen Him, time after time, smile with love at those who flocked to Him like sheep to their Shepherd, seeking one word from His lips, one touch from His hand.

She had seen Him weep at the death of a beloved friend. She had seen Him wipe away the tears and rejoice when that friend emerged from his tomb.

Impossible. That was what the religious leaders had claimed when He brought life back to the limbs of one dead four days already. That was what they said about so much that He did. *Impossible.*

Someone shoved her from behind, someone else elbowed her in the ribs. All around her, people shouted the ugliest words she had ever heard. "Crucify Him! *Crucify Him!*"

Magdalene pulled Imma Mary tighter to her side, willing her own limbs to grow so that she could better protect her from the savage reality unfurling before them. Only because Imma's head was bowed could Magdalene look over the top of it, meeting the eyes of the other Mary, mother of two of the Twelve.

They needed to break free of this horrible crowd before the screaming men trampled them. Yet *leaving* wasn't an option. They couldn't just abandon the Master now. How could they? For three years, He had ministered to their every need, their every hurt. He had filled their ears with truth that sank all the way to their souls.

He had redefined everything. He had brought light to a world dark with sin and hatred and death.

She felt it now, elbowing them as solidly as the crowd. *Evil.* Surging, boiling, frothing evil. Dark clouds of it gnashing its teeth in anticipation. Her skin prickled, her stomach churned. She had known that very evil, once. She had lived with it, had welcomed it inside her. She had nearly let it consume her.

But He had changed all that. He had cast out the demons, had banished the darkness.

What did it mean, that the darkness was back? What did it mean, that Jesus had let Himself be arrested, that He staggered even now under the weight of a Roman cross?

He could have stopped it. He could have banished this darkness as He had banished it from her soul—with a word, a touch. When He commanded it to, the darkness had no choice but to flee.

The jeering crowd surged again, their knot of women nearly falling beneath the angry feet of the Lord's accusers. They gripped one another fiercely, and Magdalene knew that they each had the same determination in their spirits that she did.

They would stay together. They would see where they took Him. They would be there, every moment, so that if He had the strength to look up and see them, He would know that He was not alone.

Jesus. Jesus! Her soul wept for Him, even though her eyes remained strangely dry. This horror was too great even for tears—tears would only blind her. Tears would put them in danger.

Imma Mary had a hand splayed over her heart as she watched her Son's progress along the long, dirt-packed road. "He warned me," she whispered. "Simeon, in the Temple. When Joseph and I presented Him to God. He warned me that my precious boy would divide Israel. He warned me that my heart would be pierced."

Magdalene had already heard the story, countless times. Each time, she had marveled at the words of prophecy that both Simeon and Anna had spoken over the newborn babe. They had known, when He was but a helpless infant in His mother's arms. They had known and had come to greet their Lord, before He ever spoke His first word.

They had known they were in the presence of God made man, wrapped in fragile human flesh.

Fragile—so fragile. She knew it when she saw other babies and marveled that He had been one too. Yet since she'd known Him, He had been anything but fragile.

He was the Healer of wounds, spiritual and mental and physical.

He was the Doer of miracles.

He was the Master of the sea and the wind.

He calmed storms.

He walked on water.

He held the laws of the world, the Laws of God, in His capable hands.

But now those hands clutched one of the rough-hewn arms of the cross they had laid upon His shoulder. Splinters pierced His palms—she could see them digging in as He trudged nearer. Obviously whoever had made that horrible torture device didn't care if it hurt its victims before it killed them. Why should he?

Yet she couldn't banish the ridiculous, unimportant thought: Jesus would have made it with more care. He would have planed each surface smooth with all the patience His earthly father, Joseph, had taught Him. Because each item they fashioned in the woodshop deserved such attention. Each was a creation that remembered the true Creation of God.

When Jesus first told that story around a campfire one night in the countryside while He whittled a stick into a toy for one of the children, Magdalene had grinned and looked to His mother. Imma Mary had been smiling too, at the memory of the husband she still mourned. At the time, Magdalene had wondered who had really taught that lesson to whom. She had wondered if, as He put small human hands to small human creations, He was remembering what it had felt like to truly create everything from nothing.

Was that thunder rumbling over the hills? The crowd?

The powers of darkness?

"This way!" she yelled to her companions when a passage opened up through the swarm of people.

She and Imma's sister led the others through the opening in the wall of people, emerging a moment later onto the edge of the road.

He would pass by here. He had no choice. Magdalene's whole self yearned for Him, even as she wished Him anywhere but here. Any time but now. In any other position.

Why? Why had He let this happen? What did it *mean*? He was the Son of God! Conceived without the seed of a man, placed in the virgin womb of this woman beside her. He was the one man in all of history who had lived a life totally pure before God. He held all power, all authority—she had seen it.

She had felt it. It had saved her from sure destruction.

Yet as she watched, He stumbled—He, whose feet had always been sure upon His path as He brought healing and the Good News of salvation to all of Judea and beyond. He fell—He, who had raised up so many who by rights should never be able to lift their own heads. His knees struck the ground—He, who had commanded the storm, withered the fig tree, told them all that they could cast the mountains into the sea.

Would He even be able to stand again? His muscles shuddered, quivered, twitched in exhaustion. As He bowed to the earth, Magdalene got her first glimpse of His back—a sight gruesome enough that she had to avert her eyes, and which elicited a groan from Imma.

She had known they were taking Him to be scourged. Knowing it hadn't prepared her for the reality of the stripes across His back. Each place the lash hit Him, His flesh had been ripped, peeled away.

He had healed so many others, countless multitudes. He had healed them of illness and disease, of injury and defect. He had cast out legions of demons.

Were they the very ones now whispering their mockery into the ears of this mob, so eager to spew them back out at Him?

The Roman soldiers yelled at Him to get up, and He tried to obey. He heaved upward, managed to lift Himself and the cross a foot, but then both crashed back down. What would they do? Apply more lashes with the whips in their hands?

No—one of the soldiers scanned the crowd on the side of the road opposite Magdalene and her companions, pointed at the tallest, broadest man he saw, and shouted something she couldn't make out.

It didn't remain a mystery for long. The man, his face a seething storm that mixed rebellion with obedience, shoved his way out of the crowd. A flicker of compassion calmed the storm.

Magdalene looked back down at Jesus for a moment, but then her gaze snapped to His compulsory helper. He looked to be about the same age her own abba would have been. And there was something familiar about him.

The height. The chiseled jaw. The strong form.

Familiar...but it couldn't be Simon, could it? No—she was only imagining the resemblance to Simon's son. She'd never even met the patriarch himself, so she certainly wouldn't recognize him. Even so, each time she looked back at him, he was *Simon* in her thoughts.

The knots in her stomach cinched tighter. If this man was anything like Simon's son, he was as likely to kick the Lord in the ribs as to lift the cross from His shoulders. She felt the fresh bruises on her arms, swore she could smell again the wine-laden breath in her face. Heard his slurred accusations stinging her ears. *"This is all your fault! You brought me here, you made me so low! Would that I had never looked on your cursed face!"*

His father didn't lash out, though, whether from his own sense of decency or because of the soldiers barking out orders. He simply knelt down beside the Lord, put his own shoulder beside His, and levered the crossbeam over onto it. He stood again as if it weighed nothing, as if he hadn't at least five decades of age on his muscles.

Now when one of the soldiers pulled Jesus to His feet, He managed to hold Himself upright, though still He swayed. How much blood had He lost? How many bruises mottled the skin she couldn't see?

At the soldier's next bark, Jesus started forward again. His gaze lifted from the road, perhaps when He heard the keening of His aunt and the other Mary, and landed on them—each of them, lingering for a moment on His mother before moving to Magdalene.

"Where is it you want to be, Mary?"

He had asked her that question several times over the years—each one, at a pivotal moment in her life. Each one solidifying her decision to follow Him. He didn't ask it now, not aloud, but she could see it in His eyes.

"Where is it you want to be, Mary?"

She held His mother tighter and lifted her wobbling chin. She would remain exactly where she had sworn to Him years ago she would be. She would follow Him even now. She would not let a moment of His life slip by without her.

His gaze moved back again, to His aunt and the other Mary. Was He wondering where their sons had gone? Why they were not here with them?

No. He knew. "Daughters of Jerusalem," He croaked, voice rough, gaze gentle and loving as it moved from one of them to the other, "don't weep for Me. Weep for yourselves. Weep for your children. For the day is coming when they will say, 'Blessed are the barren, the wombs that never bore.' Days are coming when people will beg for the earth to cover them."

And they would face it without Him? Then Magdalene would indeed wish for the hills to fall on her and cover her. She had faced life without Him before—empty years of supposed pleasure that only brought pain, of ambition that led her to scorn. Years of waste and ruin.

She wouldn't go back there again. She would *not*.

CHAPTER TWO

The floor was cool and hard beneath her cheek, the world sideways when Magdalene blinked open her eyes. Where was she? Expensive tile pressed to her side…music and laughter echoing through the corridors and making her head pound… dozens of scents warring for prominence in her nostrils and making her stomach churn.

Her villa? No. No, this wasn't Magdala. If it were, there would be no music, no laughter, no riot of smells. There would be the trickle of the fountain, the soft humming of her trusted staff, the fragrance of a simple stew mixed with that of Abba's scrolls and inks.

No stew here. No ink. No Abba.

The palace. She shifted, pressed a henna-decorated palm to the floor, and pushed herself up to sitting. Her stomach rolled, and her throat burned with bile. She must have vomited— that accounted for the acrid taste that persisted beneath the mint she must have rinsed her mouth with. It also accounted for the hollow feeling of her stomach, despite the fact that she'd have been eating for hours already, given the darkness seeping through the window high above her.

"Not again." She leaned against the wall, let her eyes slide closed, and tried to remember. She had a vague recollection of the feast—she could see Salome's imitation of a smile in her mind's eye, hear Herod announcing his stepdaughter and niece's engagement. She could remember the stir of pity in her own chest at realizing that her young friend's fears had been realized and she really would be forced to marry a man more than twice her age, all in the name of political alliances.

Salome had known it was coming. That didn't mean she liked it.

Magdalene rubbed her fingertips to her temples, searching for more wisps of memory. Something to account for why she was out here in the hallway, alone, rather than in with her friends. Something to make sense of the gap in her mind.

It was happening more and more. Minutes, sometimes hours, just *gone*. Minutes and hours that she could never account for. What had she done in these missing moments? She searched her mind again, but no more images of the feast greeted her.

Instead, those *other* memories bombarded her, as they always did. When she pushed herself to her feet, it was the tile of the villa she felt. That warm breeze from the window became the summer wind luring her out into the courtyard. The lyre and flute became the cry of birds.

No. Stop. Stop remembering. But she couldn't. She never could once her mind started down that path. No matter where her feet really were, they were back taking those dreadful steps. The ones that ended in a pool of something warm and sticky. The metallic smell of blood stung her nose. Her eyes could see only the horror that had torn her family apart.

Abba. Abba!

Stumbling over her own sluggish feet, Magdalene groped her way along the corridor of Herod's palace, trying to will her hand to steady, to force the images from her mind. She didn't want to see her father like that again, slain for…what? Had it been an attempted robbery? An assassination? Whoever did it hadn't come into the house to try to steal the bulk of their valuables, but Abba's moneybag had been missing, along with the jewelry he'd been wearing. Which meant probably not an assassination and not a well-plotted theft.

A transient ruffian, the authorities had said. Someone who had seen her father in the markets and followed him home. A crime of convenience, that was all.

All. As if it hadn't destroyed everything.

The music grew louder as she made her way along the hallway. Good. Instruments and people meant something to force these older images from her mind. When she was thinking about eating and drinking and dancing, when she was debating which rich, handsome nobleman she'd smile at next, there was no room for those other thoughts. No room for remembering Abba's lifeless body in her arms. No room in her vision for the horrified expressions on the servants' faces. No room for Rhoda's chiding in her ears.

"You can't, Mary. You're unclean. You touched his corpse."

Unclean. Even thinking the word made a shiver course through her. She needed water. Soap. Soap strong enough to scrub the memory from her skin, from her bones, from her soul. Having none, she settled for looking at her hands, at the careful henna design drawn onto them. With one finger, she traced the pattern.

"Make it go away." The whisper was familiar to her lips, each word tasting like a friend. She'd shouted it, once, at the shadows. Desperate for anything to make the constant whirl of memory halt. She'd shouted it, and she'd thrown herself into those shadows, and…she'd come to herself here then too—not in this exact hallway but in the palace. Joanna had been laughing at her side, their arms linked together.

It had taken her several minutes that first time to stitch together why she was in the palace at all. *The invitations*, she'd eventually realized. She must have accepted the invitations she always received to join the festivities at Herod's court. Joanna had been begging her to come for months before Abba's death. She must have finally listened to her old friend's pleading.

Her father had never approved of the lives of the courtiers. But the music was loud enough to drown out her screams. The feasts were regular enough to help her forget how hollow she was inside, all the time. The crush of people was big enough to disguise the fact that she had felt so very alone, utterly forsaken, for…how long had it been now?

Two years? No. Three. Three years since Abba was slain. Three years since she and her siblings had parted ways, each to their own inheritance, their condemnation slapping her in the face. Three years since she'd set aside the modest ways of the Jews and embraced what her brother, Azur, had called the "pagan hedonism" of Herod's court.

"Magdalene!" The familiar voice preceded the appearance of Joanna from around a corner, concern in her eyes but a smile still clinging to her lips. She was dressed much like Magdalene, in the finest of fabrics dyed to a rich hue, gold adorning her wrists, throat, ears, and nose. Joanna had married Khuza five years ago, and she had never made a secret of enjoying the life she lived as wife of Herod's steward. *She* certainly never seemed bothered by the condemnation of the Jews who saw one of their own in Roman dress and declared her a traitor.

Magdalene straightened her spine and tried to paste a matching smile onto her lips. She tried to portray the image Joanna had helped her craft—wealthy, sophisticated, independent woman. No longer *Mary*, youngest of three siblings, daughter of a Jewish merchant. Now she was *Magdalene*, a woman whose unique position as heir to the villa that reigned over Magdala meant that she was more than another Jewish daughter.

If only she could convince herself of that. She grasped the hand Joanna held out. "It happened again. I have no idea how I ended up out here."

One short, fearful flicker in her friend's eyes, and then Joanna waved it off and laughed. "You had too much wine again, clearly."

"I didn't." Did she? Maybe she had. She had no recollection of how many times the servants had refilled her cup. "Or perhaps I did. How is Salome?"

"Smiling and laughing as though this betrothal had been all her idea." Joanna linked their arms together and led Magdalene around a corner. The music doubled in volume with that one turn.

Yes. Blessed, blessed noise to drown out all the memories. A few of the shadows retreated. Or perhaps swirled around her? She didn't know anymore, but that was all right. The flute made her blood trill, and the beat of the drum made it pulse. This was the closest she ever came to feeling alive.

They slipped back into the banquet hall, and Magdalene's eyes scanned the crowd. *There,* the two women who were her biggest rivals in wealth and beauty—Flavia and Porcia. Flavia had dared to wear purple tonight, and Herodias had been glaring at her all night. Everyone knew that *she,* Herod's wife, was the only one who should appear in purple at one of her husband's feasts, unless she invited someone else to do the same. Tonight, of course, Salome had been given leave to join her mother in her splendor.

But that Flavia had sought to eclipse the royal ladies? Scandalous. She would no doubt feel the bite of the princess's hatred for the overstep, and Magdalene didn't envy her the war to come. Herodias could be vindictive and cruel, never letting a slight go unpunished.

She could also be patient, waiting weeks or months or even years to exact her revenge.

No, Magdalene had learned her lesson about Herodias early—stay always on her good side, always in her shadow. That was how one advanced in Herod's court.

Porcia knew the lesson Flavia had flaunted. She was arguably wealthier than Herod himself after her husband died and left her with everything, but she always played the role of doting devotee to Herodias. Although at the moment, she was too busy flirting with a toga-bedecked man to notice that the princess was trying to get her attention.

Well. Magdalene saw, and perhaps Herodias would be as happy to have *her* answer the summons as Porcia. After extracting her arm from Joanna's with a wink, she quickly moved to the head table and dipped to her knees at the princess's side. "My lady. May I assist you?"

"I'm glad *someone* is paying attention. Thank you, Magdalene, yes. My daughter seems to have gotten lost coming back from seeing to her personal needs. Would you be so kind as to remind her of her way?"

Best not to mention that *she* had lost her way a bit too. "Of course, my lady. It would be my pleasure." She stood, bowed her head in respect to Herod when he glanced her way, and hurried away from the thrones.

Joanna intercepted her on her way to the door opposite the one they'd just come in through. "Looking for Salome?"

Magdalene smiled. Joanna always kept her finger on the pulse of the royal household—everyone knew that Khuza was so successful as a steward in large part because of his lovely young wife. "Did you see where she went?"

"Her usual hiding place."

No surprise there. They wound their way through the crowd, smiling and issuing greetings as they went. Magdalene felt the gazes of several different men following her but ignored them all for now.

If only Joanna would have as well. She leaned close, conspiracy in her tone as she said, "I do believe Archelaus is studying you rather intently. He clearly approves of how we styled your hair tonight."

Magdalene tucked a tendril behind her ear, her fingers brushing against the long strand of pearls Joanna had instructed the maids to use to bind Magdalene's thick, waist-length locks. Her friend always claimed that her hair was her crowning glory, too beautiful to be covered as Jewish tradition dictated.

Here in the palace, few women observed that tradition anyway. They dressed in the Roman style, and Roman women never covered their hair. They adorned it, braided it, showed it off. Was it rebellion that had made her want to do the same? Vanity? Pride? A desire to fit in with the royal household?

It hardly mattered. Whatever her murky motivations had been, her siblings would have labeled them sin. And regardless, they had long ago faded to mere habit.

They slipped out a side door and padded softly up the stairs that led to the roof, where Salome always went for a few moments of quiet during a feast. They found her exactly as Magdalene had expected—leaning on the half wall, her pretty young face tilted up to the star-studded sky, head inclined as she listened to the music wafting up to her from below.

Magdalene slid up to the wall on one side of her, Joanna on the other. Neither of them said anything. They just rested their arms against the wall too and looked out into the night. Listened to the music and the laughter.

After a minute of shared silence, Salome sighed. "My mother sent you?"

"She was concerned you lost your way." Magdalene knew her amusement with the obvious excuse came through in her tone.

"I was tempted to lose my way all the way back to my bed-chamber." She drew in a long breath and turned away from the sky. What did she see when she looked out at it? Freedom? The fates governing her life? The heavens of the Jewish God? All Magdalene ever saw were the stars that had mocked her as they counted out the seven days she'd been called unclean after she cradled her father's lifeless body in her arms. Seven days when she couldn't join the rest of the family in their grieving, in their meals, in their preparations. Seven days that had managed to sever her from the life she'd once known.

Unclean. Unclean.

She rubbed a hand over her opposite arm. Gold encircled her wrist; henna ink danced in beautiful patterns from her palms to her elbows. The edge of silk brushed her forearm. But it was blood she felt there still. Abba's blood, Abba's life, staining her. A shiver overtook her.

Salome tilted her face toward Magdalene. "Are you chilled? I thought it a pleasant evening."

She pasted a smile onto her lips. Salome wasn't like her mother—one could disagree with her without fearing for one's reputation—but it was her very sweetness that made sure no one ever *wanted* to disagree. "It's very pleasant indeed. I daresay my little chill wasn't from the air."

"Perhaps a ghost passed before your tomb." Joanna said it in a spooky voice, waving her fingers in the air.

Magdalene laughed. "Doubtless. I can think of no more reasonable explanation." As her laughter faded, though, she cast a glance toward the hills. The tomb that held her father,

her mother, her grandparents. The tomb that would no doubt hold her someday too. She once feared that cave and all it represented. Funny how, lately, she nearly longed for it.

A minute later, the crowds of the feast beat back any such longing for coolness and darkness and silence, for a cessation of all the missing moments, the itch of blood long since dried and washed away, the depths that seemed to swallow her one moment and vomit her back out the next. Tonight—she would focus on tonight. This feast, these people.

That man, perhaps—Archelaus, cousin of the Herod brothers. Rich and powerful and handsome, and looking at her as though she were the delicacy he meant to enjoy for dessert. His gaze swept over her as she led Salome back to Herodias's side, lingering in each and every place her belted stola invited him to do so.

Then began the dance. He came closer, moving around a cluster of laughing nobles, eyes still focused on her. She sidestepped, putting another group between them but casting a half smile over her shoulder. *Come and chase me.*

Run away, Mary. The voice, small and panicked, was as familiar and as distant as the child she'd once been.

She lifted a chalice of wine from the tray of a passing servant, twirled around a couple staggering from their own drink toward the door, and met Archelaus's gaze as she took a sip. *Drink of my lips. Love me.*

The wine, spiced and watered, churned in her stomach. *He'll never love you, Mary. None of these men will ever love you.*

But maybe he would. Maybe this one, this man, this time would be unlike all the others. Maybe to him she'd be more than long hair and womanly curves and a lovely face. Maybe he'd see…see…

What? What have you left them to see? You're dead inside. Dead like Abba. Dead like Imma.

Panic burned like bile in her throat. She—that voice of her past—was right.

No, hissed another voice in her ear. *You will find someone to love you. You will find fame and security and wealth. All this will be yours. And pleasure. Pleasure beyond your wildest dreams.*

Her hands shook as she set the chalice down on a table and moved to a window, greedy for fresh air.

A moment later, though, she felt him draw near. One hand trailed down the pearl-bound length of her hair, the other settled at her waist, and his mouth took up position at her ear, right where that voice had hissed. "Mary of Magdala, isn't it? The fame of your beauty precedes you."

Pull away. Go back to your room. Leave this place, leave!

She turned, fully resolved in that moment to obey herself. Only, her limbs wouldn't listen. She watched her hand lift, toy with the gather of his toga at his shoulder. She felt her lips curl into a temptress's smile. And she heard her voice, hers but not issued at her own command, say, "Call me Magdalene."

CHAPTER THREE

Magdalene blinked awake, wishing even as she did so that she hadn't. Reaching mental fingers out toward that blissful haze of sleep and willing it back again. Trying for one more hour or minute or even second to cling to the oblivion.

Sunlight stabbed her in the eyes with that first blink, though, assaulting her every sense. She winced, rolled away from the window, and tried not to groan. Once, she'd loved mornings. Morning had meant more time to laugh with her siblings, to joke with her abba, to see what delights the world would bring her that day.

Now, mornings always meant a churning stomach, aching body, and hazy regret. What had she done last night? Did she even dare to probe her memory?

No. Better not to. Better to simply get on with today. She pushed herself up, wincing at the change in altitude, and rubbed a hand over her eyes. Her fingers came away smudged with the kohl she apparently hadn't washed off last night.

She stared at the silver-black smudges. An apt image of her life. Black smears over what once had been clean. The weight of it all settled on her shoulders so that she very nearly let it push her back into the bed she always called her own when she stayed at the palace. That wouldn't solve anything though.

She could have called for a servant to help her clean up and dress for the day, but she wasn't ready to face another person yet. Better to drift over to the window once she gained her feet and look out at the countryside. Magdala was there, on the next hill. The land between the village and the larger town around Herod's palace was lush with vineyards. *Her* vineyards. She would walk through them later, check the vines' health, examine the leaves for spot and blight.

And what would she do if she found some? What would she do if this year's harvest failed? Or if her next review of the ledgers showed her that her steward was cheating her? It wasn't impossible—Abba had dismissed a steward for that when she was a girl. She'd listened at the door as he ran through the litany of complaints against the man. Barnabas hadn't shown any of the same faults so far, but that didn't mean he wouldn't.

How fragile it all was. Her whole world could come tumbling down with one bad year, one dishonest servant. Then what would become of her? Without the money from her property, she couldn't afford the life she lived here. And everyone would know. They would know and they would pick her apart until she was nothing but dried-up bones.

She leaned into the open window frame, running a fingertip under her eye to wipe away yesterday's kohl. She'd go home today, that was all. She would examine the records again. Meet with Barnabas. And the vinedresser too, just to see how the crop was doing. She would make sure everything was as it should be. She would remind them all that she kept as firm a hand on the reins as Abba ever had.

Firmer. *She* didn't have to divide her attention between this estate and the one outside Jerusalem that her brother now ran. Her whole focus was given to the villa and vineyard here, and it would thrive. It would grow. It would prove to the world, to the court, to the shadows in her own soul that Abba hadn't made a mistake when he left the property to her. She was the mistress. The heiress.

She was Magdalene. Lady of Magdala.

She was going to throw up. She ran for the basin beside her bed, though only dry heaves met her. Still, it made her face flush, heat and cold taking turns rippling over her body.

The knock that sounded on her door pierced her head like stakes, bringing a snarl to her lips. "Go away!"

Instead, the door opened and Joanna—who never drank more than two cups of wine—laughed her way inside like the horrible, mocking creature she was. Her eyes, clean and fresh and bright as the sun, sparkled at her. "I've come to relieve your morning mood. Are you fretting over your estate still, or have you moved on to whether Herodias will realize you're too pretty and exile you from court?"

The only possible answer was to pick up the closest thing at hand—one of her sandals—and lob it at Joanna's head. Or in her general direction, anyway. It hit the wall, nowhere even close to where her friend laughed anew.

"I see—you're in the 'why did I have that last cup of wine?' stage. Though really, Magdalene…" She frowned and moved around the rumpled bed, the sandal in hand. "You shouldn't be so bad off. You only had one cup after your visit to the vomitorium, and you ate with it."

Had she? A flash of an image filled her mind—Archelaus feeding her a bite of something dripping honey and almonds. But it was only a sliver of a memory. She shook it away. "Perhaps it was the food that didn't agree with me. Or perhaps it's the morning itself."

"Well, I have the remedy for whatever it is." Joanna dropped the sandal next to its match and propelled Magdalene toward the dressing table and stool, pushing her down so that she was looking into the polished silver mirror.

She winced at the sight that greeted her. Much as she wanted to chalk it up to the foggy, imperfect reflection, she knew better. If anything, the mirror softened reality. "I am definitely not worried about Herodias growing jealous of me this morning."

Joanna chuckled and handed her a damp washcloth. The water was warm, which meant a servant had been in recently to fill her basin. She added a dab of oil to the cloth to help remove the cosmetics and refresh her skin and gently wiped her eyes, then folded the cloth and cleansed the rest of her face.

Better. Much better. Not just in appearance, but the light fragrance of the oil improved her mood too. "What is your supposed remedy? I really need to return to Magdala today and—"

"Intimidating poor Barnabas can wait until tomorrow." Joanna darted over to the trunk that held the clothing Magdalene kept at the palace and started digging through it. "Herod has some special entertainment planned for us this morning."

She didn't bother stifling her groan. "Let me guess—another pitiful, boring prisoner to parade before us. Who will it be this time? A lunatic to growl and rave and try to break free of his chains? A zealot captured in the hills, half-mad from starvation? No, I know—"

"I highly doubt it." Joanna tossed a fresh tunic at her and then held up two stolas for her to choose between.

Magdalene motioned to the pale blue one on the right. "All right then. Who?"

"A *prophet*." Joanna's amber eyes were wide as she pronounced it, her curls bouncing along with the rest of her.

Magdalene frowned and took her clothing with her behind the screen. "Why does Herod have a prophet as a prisoner?"

"If I were to guess, he didn't like his prophecies. Though, come now, he can't be a *real* prophet, can he? There are none anymore, if ever there were. Everyone knows that. The days of Daniel or Isaiah or Samuel are long gone. The God of Abraham has gone silent—or at least has been distilled down to the rules and regulations that the Sanhedrin so loves to oppress us with."

The words made unease dig talons into Magdalene's shoulder blades. She had never been the pious girl her sister, Sarah, was. She had never really thought of their God as anything but a driving force who lived far beyond their reach…but she had a healthy fear of Him. Abba had worshiped the Lord as the Law dictated he should—for all the good it did him—and had always spoken of Him with reverence.

She could never quite get used to Joanna saying such things. But then, she suspected that was why Joanna did it—to try to get someone to argue with her. "Abba always said the Lord spoke *through* the Law, just as He did through the Prophets."

"And what does He say? That we are all wretched, that there's nothing we can ever do to be perfect as He is perfect? If ever we get close, He piles on new rules. I've had enough of them. I'll obey the rule of Caesar, I'll obey my husband. But no invisible deity can tell me how to live my life."

Magdalene slipped the fine linen tunic on and then reached for the softly draping stola. "Nor one of His prophets? Is that why you're so pleased with the morning's entertainment?"

This time, Joanna's laugh sounded tarnished. "Maybe. Or maybe part of me wants this one to be real. Maybe I'm hoping that if I taunt God enough, He'll show Himself."

"And there we have the truth of the matter." Magdalene pulled the weight of her hair from under her clothing and stepped back out. Seeing the bittersweet look on her friend's face, she had to sigh and reach out a hand. "God doesn't show Himself to the likes of us, Joanna. We are only women—sinful ones. From what I recall from the Chronicles, if the prophet is true and looks upon us, it would only be to condemn us like Jezebel."

Joanna wrinkled her nose. "We're not as bad as all that. I personally haven't ordered any prophets of the Lord put to death in all my life. Nor worshiped Ba'al—I don't even make offerings to the Roman gods. Does that count for nothing in the eyes of the Lord?"

As if she knew any better than Joanna? Magdalene shrugged and moved back over to the small table so she could pick up her hairbrush and work it through the tangles. "Perhaps. Mostly, I have to think it matters nothing at all. Who are we, to gain the attention of the Almighty God?"

She said the words lightly, flippantly. But they settled on her tongue after she spoke them and, when she swallowed, seemed to travel down her throat and make a fist around her heart. God hadn't seen Abba, to save him. He hadn't seen their family, to hold them together. He would never see Magdalene either. The only favor she would ever find was what she could grab for herself—from her neighbors, her servants, Herod's court, whatever man she eventually decided to wed.

An eventuality that she didn't much want to consider, but which would prove more fruitful to think about than an ever-distant God. The man she married would gain control of all that was hers, all Abba had left to her. The man she married would become her lord and king as surely the tetrarch or the emperor. The man she married would no doubt stop using words of love and praising her beauty and do what all men seemed to do: control her.

Had Abba been different with Imma? She didn't remember her mother well enough to know, hadn't thought to pay any attention to their relationship. She only knew what she saw everywhere she looked now, and that was a world where, unless a woman asserted herself like Herodias, she ended up one more possession.

Joanna gusted out a sigh of her own and picked through the box of jewelry still out from last night. "You're always so depressing in the morning."

Because morning never brought anything but pain. "Why is it depressing to think we'll avoid the attention of God? I rather like it that way. His attention is a fearsome thing."

The tilt of Joanna's head may have been agreement, or perhaps acknowledgment. Or maybe she was just making her final decision on what necklace Magdalene should wear, because she slid one out of the box and draped it around her neck for her. "I suppose you have a point. Herod's attention is certainly fearsome enough, and he is but a man."

"Mm. At least Khuza dotes on you. Who needs God when you have a husband who is in love with you?"

Joanna's smile looked rather smug. "Another good point you've made."

Her hair was as smooth as it was going to get. She debated braiding it to keep it from her face, but the continual throb at her temples lured her into letting it hang free instead. She stood. "All right. Let's go be entertained, shall we?"

Together they made their way through the palace's maze of guest rooms and small gathering places, arriving at last at the throne room.

Archelaus stood at the door—the first test of whether his affections were fleeting as the wind. Would he look at her? Try to woo her?

He glanced their way, clearly saw her, but made not the slightest sign of greeting or even of recognition. He simply kept talking to the scribe beside him.

What had she expected? Hoped for? That she had meant something more to him than he had to her?

Her stomach, still so unsettled, felt heavy as lead as she brushed past him. She could barely even summon up a smile for Gaius—one of the men who never dreamed of ignoring her—as he approached her, looking utterly delighted at her presence.

"Magdalene! The sun shows its brilliant face on the day at last." He took her hand, sliding a gold bangle onto her wrist as he did so. "I got this from a man in the caravan that arrived yesterday and knew it could adorn no wrist but yours, my dearest one."

Sweet Gaius. She smiled, learning long ago that it was pointless to refuse his gifts. She'd tried a few times, but they always ended up among her things thanks to whatever servant he bribed to put them there. She paid him the compliment of studying the truly outstanding piece of goldwork. "It's stunning, Gaius. Where did your people find such a craftsman?"

"Oh, somewhere in Egypt, I believe. If anyone asks where you found it, direct them to my people."

"Of course." And that was all she really was to the sweet old man—a model for his merchandise. Having delivered his latest gift, he took his leave too.

"This way." Joanna led her through the crowd, around to the thrones positioned at the front of the room and the rows of cushions around them. They chose their positions near to Salome and Herodias, as usual.

Porcia joined them a moment later, her gaze focused on something opposite them. "Who is *that*, Joanna? Do you know?"

Magdalene followed her nod too, not needing to ask for clarification on whom Porcia meant. There was only one stranger in the area indicated—a man of perhaps thirty, with a head of gleaming dark hair, a well-chiseled face, and a piercing gaze focused on their group as surely as theirs was on him. Magdalene's throat went dry.

Joanna leaned close. "His name is Alexander, I believe. He just arrived from Cyrene a few days ago. He's the son of a very wealthy merchant, one of the Jewish families who have been living in Africa since the dispersion."

He was handsome. Young. Well positioned. Maybe he would be kind. Attentive. Maybe he would see more than her beauty. Maybe he would be the one to make life take on meaning again.

He started toward them, and Magdalene's pulse picked up even as Porcia let out a quiet squeal of delight. He could be the one. The one to change everything. The one to make her *feel* something again. He could be the one worthy of trusting with all she had, with her heart, with her future.

A trumpet sounded, sending everyone into a flurry that ended in stillness. A moment later a voice cried out, "Before his royal majesty, Herod Antipas, his esteemed wife, Herodias, and all the royal court, the condemned prisoner is brought forth—the one known as John, the Baptizer."

The…*Baptizer*? Magdalene searched her mind, trying to pinpoint why that sounded familiar. Hadn't she heard talk of him when last she was in Jerusalem? Yes, that was it—he had the religious leaders in an uproar with all his talk of repentance. Parades of citizens had apparently joined him at the Jordan for this baptizing he promoted, plunging themselves into the water as if it could really make them new. As if their lives were changed a whit when they came up again.

She'd never seen this supposed prophet, but she'd heard he was a wild man. Unkempt, filthy. Likely a lunatic.

A rattle of chains, and two guards escorted the prisoner into the court, halting him before the royal family, and hence not far from Magdalene. She drew in a breath. Unkempt, yes. His hair was long, his beard frazzled. His clothing was utterly ridiculous—was the cloth made of…camel hide? Yes, camel hair and a leather belt.

He smelled, but that was to be expected after a few days in prison. Magdalene didn't wrinkle her nose like her friends did, though, nor did she pull out a perfumed handkerchief. That would have required looking away.

And looking away was, in that moment, unthinkable.

CHAPTER FOUR

Herod leaned forward, into Magdalene's peripheral vision. "Your name is John? From the region of Galilee?"

The prisoner lifted his head. "I am John. The voice in the wilderness. Sent to proclaim to all who will listen that they must repent—for the kingdom of God is at hand!"

All around her, laughter erupted. "Repent!" many echoed, as if the word itself was the greatest jest ever given utterance, more laughter following their mockery.

"Kingdom of *God*, he says." This came from behind her, a man who snorted over the words. "Whoever would have thought it—a Jewish prophet declaring Caesar is God! For his is the only kingdom *I* see!"

Magdalene had to bite her tongue to keep from turning around and shushing the one who had said it. Though Herodias sent a scathing look over her shoulder, no doubt at the reminder that the Herodian dynasty was subject to Rome.

"Lunatic," Porcia muttered at her side.

Magdalene shook her head. She had seen her share of madmen brought before the tetrarch for his entertainment. Men with wild eyes or vague ones, some whose words were incomprehensible. This John, despite his appearance, didn't seem crazed at all. The eyes he sent around the room were intelligent, lucid…piercing. When his gaze brushed over her, a shiver danced down her spine, and something within her recoiled. Something else leaned forward. One part screamed for him to be silent, another waited for his next words like a desert animal awaited the dewfall.

Repent. She knew the word, of course. It had simply never meant anything to her. How exactly did one even accomplish it?

She tore her gaze away from the Baptizer so that she could gauge the royal family's reaction to him. Herod was still leaning forward, a half smile on his lips. But was that simple amusement in his eyes or something deeper? Was he intrigued? It was difficult to say without seeing him directly.

Herodias's response was less questionable. She wore boredom upon her face without any softening mask, and her arms were folded across her chest.

The prisoner was studying the couple as well. "Mocking the Lord of Hosts is unwise. I suppose, though, that I should not be surprised you would do it. Have not the people of this court, and especially the house of Herod, mocked the Lord in every part of your lives?"

More shouts and laughter from the gallery, some tinged now with outrage. Odd, that—she had never heard most of these people even admit to believing in the God of Abraham, so why were they offended at being accused of mocking Him?

Herod leaned back a few inches. "How, pray, have I mocked the Lord? Am I not the duly appointed ruler of His people?"

Duly appointed by Caesar rather than God—would John point that out? Was that the mockery he spoke of, that Herod dared to sit on the throne without being of the lineage of David?

But the man's gaze had moved for some reason to Herodias. "You mock Him every time you take your brother's wife to your bed. You have wed an unholy woman, one who dared to divorce her husband. You sin against God, against your own flesh and blood, and against all the people you are supposed to lead."

"What?" Herodias's attention no longer strayed. Her gaze had snapped forward, and her arms had gone from bored disinterest to ready to attack. She dug her nails into the arms of her throne. "You dare to call me unholy?"

John didn't so much as flinch. "It is God who dares. It is you who flout His Law. You are an adulteress, queen of adulteresses. Like the kings of old, the two of you are leading God's people into sin and abomination. Look around you!" He spread his arms wide, encompassing them all, his gaze raking over them again.

Magdalene's stomach tightened and felt sick.

"A court of vipers, ready to attack each other for the chance to advance. A court of sinners, willing to lose their souls in the pursuit of a fleeting moment's pleasure. A court of fools, seeking wealth in the kingdom of men when they could be chasing after eternal life in the kingdom of heaven!"

Porcia made a little gasping sound. "How dare he?"

A question being muttered and shouted all over the room.

Not from Magdalene's lips. She couldn't have spoken had she tried. What words could she possibly say? How could she pluck any from the whirlwind of them battering her mind?

One part of her cried, *I'm sorry! I don't want to be this way!* But another hiss silenced it. *This is the only way to survive. Everything could fall apart at any moment—what would you have left without these alliances?*

It doesn't matter what you do. Nothing matters. You're a worm, you are dust, just like your father.

Vipers! Yes, these people are vipers. Any one of them could turn on you at any moment. Even the ones you think are your friends. And the men? Their words of flattery and devotion will dry up in a flash when they see who you really are.

Nothing. You are nothing. Like your father.

Dirty. Unclean. Filthy.

She squeezed her eyes shut against the torrent. Then opened them again when those dreadful images of Abba, slain, tried to fill her mind's eye. *No.* Not now.

Shadows crept into the edges of her visions. Those familiar, growing shadows that would close over her at any moment. That would blind her to the world around her, eclipse her senses. They would make it all go away, at least for a little while.

No! Not now. She wouldn't give in, not *now.* As much as the Baptizer's words scored her heart, the blood that dripped out felt...*alive.* Warm, where she'd been so cold. Full, where she'd been so empty. Real, where she'd been only a vapor for so long.

The Baptizer. Her hands itched for cleansing water, for soap, for something to remove the stain. Water had always failed her though. It washed away Abba's blood, but it hadn't made her clean. Only time, the prescribed seven endless days, had done that.

What then of her sin? What could wash *that* away? Water couldn't do it. What, then? Time? Sacrifice? Blood?

She shuddered and pressed a hand to her mouth, afraid that the knot of nausea in her stomach would work its way up.

"Is it your pride that stings?" John sent the words out over the crowd, raising his shackled hands. "Or is it your conscience? Let it awaken within you! There is hope. Repent, I say. Turn from your wicked ways and the Lord will have mercy."

Mercy. No one had ever shown her mercy, not since that terrible day. The thief who killed her father had shown none; the Law that had separated her unclean hands from her family in the moment when she most needed to embrace them had shown none. Her brother and sister had shown none.

And if they didn't, how could God?

More, if God would condemn Herod and Herodias, when the laws of man didn't apply to them, how could this man speak of hope for the rest of them? Magdalene had no crown to protect her. No anointing to insulate her from divine justice.

If they were condemned, how much more was she?

Joanna's fingers landed on her arm, warm and secure. An anchor. "Magdalene? Are you all right?" she whispered.

Magdalene drew a long, slow breath in through her nose. She managed a nod—it may have been a lie, but it was a necessary one. She could neither fall to pieces here in the court nor admit that she'd been shattered long ago, barely held together by ambition and willpower and Joanna's friendship.

From the throne, Herod's voice whipped out. "Tread carefully, man. I hold your life in my hands."

She had never seen a smile like the one John gave. Perfect peace. No concern whatsoever. "You can do only what the Lord gives you leave to do. If I perish, I perish—still I will speak truth. And the truth is that all in this room are sinners. All will face the wrath of God if you do not turn your hearts to Him and to the One He has sent."

The One He has sent? Was he speaking of himself?

Herodias snorted. "You, you mean?"

"Nay—I am but a voice calling in the wilderness. There comes One after me whose sandals I am not fit to loose."

Someone else following in this man's footsteps? Someone even more of what he was? Magdalene nearly shuddered again. Such a man would be terrifying.

"Humble—interesting." Herod waved a hand toward the guards. "Go now—but perhaps I will hear more from you later."

Only because she sat so close to the royal women did Magdalene hear Herodias's biting whisper. "Not if I have anything to say about it. Calling me an adulteress!"

Magdalene let her gaze follow the prisoner back out. He'd only been in their presence for a few minutes, but she had a feeling it would take her all day to push his words from her mind.

Once he and his guards had vanished, Magdalene stood, pulling Joanna with her. That had taken so little time, she could still make it home today after all. "I think I'll return to Magdala. Did you want to come?"

Joanna was looking past her, and her expression was bright with conspiracy. "Oh, I don't think you want to leave quite yet,

Magdalene. Unless you want to leave the newcomer to Porcia. He's coming this way."

Newcomer? It took her a moment—and a pivot of her head—to realize that her friend meant Alexander of Cyrene, not John the Baptizer. He was indeed striding toward them, his own face intent.

Was that a thrill of excitement, or dread? She was all a muddle now, thanks to John's words. She needed quiet to sort through her own thoughts, and the walk to her villa would provide it.

Clearly that would have to wait at least a few minutes though—Alexander was nearly upon them. Perhaps Porcia had been the one to garner his attention?

Though his gaze, as he drew up to them, latched upon Magdalene, and it was she who received his smile. Something that would have sparked one of her own even a quarter of an hour ago. Now, it was all she could do to keep from spinning and snubbing him altogether.

"Forgive me for intruding—and for being forward. But are you by chance Mary of Magdala?" His voice was a baritone as smooth and rich as honey.

Beside her, Porcia huffed. Joanna, however, smiled like a proud imma. "She is. Magdalene, allow me to introduce Alexander Bar-Simon, recently of Cyrene."

His smile grew, and it looked genuine, joyful. "How fortuitous that I happened across you so soon after my arrival. You, my lady, are my primary reason for having journeyed to Israel."

"I…beg your pardon?" A bit of the urgency inside her faded, a bit of the unease relaxed. What did it really matter if she didn't leave the palace this very moment, after all? Quiet and introspection could wait a few minutes.

And he was *very* handsome, especially when he grinned as he was doing now. "Our fathers had business dealings some five years ago. It seems that they became such good friends that they'd begun to speak of…well, my lady, of a betrothal. Between their youngest children—me, for my father's part. And you, I believe."

Her throat went dry but in a totally different way than it had earlier. "A betrothal? My father mentioned nothing about it to me."

Alexander's cheeks flushed a bit. "Oh, it was nothing official. They were sounding each other out, I believe, and were going to discuss it when next they met in person. But it seems that day never came. First my mother fell ill, which kept our family from making our annual pilgrimage to Jerusalem for Passover, and then…" He cleared his throat, and his eyes softened. "I was in Rome when my father received the word, belatedly, about your father's death. He was heartsick to hear of it."

Anyone who knew him shared that pain. Abba had been such a good man. Magdalene could only manage a nod. If she tried to speak, tears would clog her throat, she knew.

After a moment's heavy pause, Alexander continued. "When I returned home to Cyrene last year, Father begged me to make the journey here, to see what became of your family. I had to wait for spring, of course, but what a relief it is to have found you so quickly. I will be able to write to my father with a happy heart to let him know you're well. And your siblings?"

She wasn't about to admit that they hadn't spoken to her—or she to them—in years. "They are well—and managing the estates closer to Jerusalem. The villa of Magdala is in my care."

Nothing flashed in his eye, neither intrigue at the knowledge nor sudden interest. Because it meant nothing to him? Or because he already knew?

He inclined his head toward her, as if listening to her thoughts. "Father knew your abba meant it to be your inheritance. It is why I came first here, rather than going directly to Jerusalem. I admit, my lady, that I longed to meet you."

Based only on her father's stories, recounted to him by his own? A long-cold piece of her heart warmed a bit, unfurling like the petals of a flower. She didn't know what Abba had said about her, but it must have been glowing. "I cannot imagine what exaggerated tales he told, to have garnered such lasting attention. Although..." The flower froze again. Five years ago—of course. "No doubt he spoke of me instead of my older sister because Sarah was already betrothed. Her bridegroom died just a few months before my father, however. If it's a match you seek, convention—"

"I've never been much for convention." His gaze warmed, sweeping her face in a way so familiar yet not quite like what other men did. "It's you I wanted to meet...Magdalene? Is that what I should call you?"

She nodded, her pulse kicking up. This couldn't actually be happening, could it? This handsome, well-positioned man, whose father had been a friend of hers, couldn't possibly have traveled so far just to make her acquaintance.

Joanna linked her arm through Magdalene's, her smile all but sparkling. "Magdalene was just saying how she needs to return to Magdala this afternoon to check on her estate. Perhaps you would be so kind as to escort her? It would give you a chance to get to know each other."

It would give him a chance to see the estate she would bring to a marriage, her friend meant. And she had a point. Magdalene's stomach fluttered with anticipation rather than nausea. "I would be delighted to have your company, if you have no other obligations."

Alexander bowed. "I am at your disposal, my lady. It would be an honor to offer the protection of myself and my guards for the walk to your villa."

She had her own guards, of course, but no need to point that out. Instead she finally smiled, taking a bit of satisfaction in the way his gaze sparked when she did so. "Well, then. Let's be on our way, shall we?"

CHAPTER FIVE

FRIDAY

Where were they? The Twelve, the ones who were supposed to be closest to Him? Magdalene kept one arm around Imma Mary's waist as they followed the Lord at a distance. Had the crowds permitted, they would have stayed closer to Him.

Perhaps it was better this way, though. Imma did not need to see the blood seeping from her Son's wounds or hear Him struggling for breath on the climb to the Place of the Skull. She had seen plenty already—she would see more to come. Perhaps this was a reprieve for her. For them all.

Magdalene searched each face of the crowd, praying for the sight of familiar ones. She knew her brother and sister were even now talking to every friend they still had, calling upon each follower of the Lord's—open or secret—to beg them for help on His behalf.

But where were the Twelve? They should be here! They should be lending their strength and support to their Master, instead of…what? Cowering in fear somewhere, afraid they'd be arrested too?

If that had been the Sanhedrin's goal, they would have seized the lot of them last night. The three in the garden. The eight who had lingered at their lodgings.

The one who had betrayed Him.

Judas. She should have been angrier with him than any of them. How could he have done it? How could he have sold his Master to His enemies? His words from last night filtered into her mind—words about forcing the Lord's hand, forcing Him to declare Himself and His kingdom, wrench Israel free from Rome.

If that had been his hope, he must now be disappointed. It looked as though Rome had won, as Rome always did.

Judas. Her eyes slid closed for a moment as she remembered his face last night. So many times she'd seen him over the years, and more often than not, he'd looked upon her like she was scum stuck to the bottom of the Master's shoe that he'd have loved to scrape off.

Maybe she was, by rights. But the Lord had been so gracious, always so gracious. He'd let her cling to Him despite her unworthiness. No, more than that—He'd told her that she *was* worthy, through the grace of God.

Last night, something new had been in Judas's eyes. Something haunted. Something sorrowful. Something that begged for forgiveness.

She hadn't known what he needed forgiveness for, at the time. And now that she did, forgiveness was the last thing she wanted to offer him.

Judas had saved her from bodily harm last night.

Without the Lord, though, she had no hope for her soul. How could she ever forgive Judas for taking that away from her? From them all?

"So many things," Imma murmured as they walked. Her steps were strong, and Magdalene could feel her determination pulling her, pulling them all, onward. Rarely had she been separated from her Son in life, and she must especially want to keep it from happening now. "So many things I stored away to ponder. Bits of treasure that I would take out and wonder about." Nostrils flaring, she shook her head. "Never did I anticipate this."

Magdalene squeezed, hoping that if she had a drop of comfort inside her, it would transfer to Jesus's mother. "How could you have?" What mother ever envisioned her fine, strong son marching toward His own crucifixion?

She wanted to be able to say it would all be all right. Somehow it would work out. That Jesus would call down angelic salvation in the last moment and destroy all His enemies in a flash of glory.

He could. She knew He could. Just as He could have done it in the garden last night, or at the trial, or when the soldiers of the garrison had pressed that horrible crown into His brow. He could have…but He hadn't.

Why? Her soul cried out the question with every heavy step. *Why, why, why?*

THREE YEARS EARLIER

Magdalene hummed as she watched her maids at work in the silver mirror—one working on her hair while another applied her cosmetics with a careful hand. She'd only tumbled out of bed an hour ago, but today wouldn't be a lazy day, nor one for understatement. They were three days into the weeklong feast celebrating Herod's birthday, and every day was its own festival. Every day the tetrarch's guests slept only enough to rise again and continue the feasting, the dancing, the drinking.

Until Alexander's arrival last month, she'd been dreading this week. There would be too much wine. Too many forgotten moments. Too many trips to the vomitorium. Too many men gazing at her with lust, reaching for her, whispering empty promises into her ears.

There would be too many mornings full of pain and regret.

Alexander had changed everything though. *Everything.* With his doting attention, the other men kept their distance. She'd been so intent upon learning all she could about him that things like food and drink had been neglected rather than overindulged. Even those blank moments had been few and far between.

Finally, *finally,* life was going according to plan. She'd found the man who would give her what the others had all lied about. The man her own father had chosen for her! She'd never even thought to dream of such a thing.

If she married him, it would solve everything. She wouldn't have to worry so much about the estate, with a man to take care of it. He wouldn't have to work so hard to earn the respect of the stewards and vinedressers. He would see to all of that, and to her as well. Someone to care for her would be a delightful change of pace. With his love secured, she wouldn't have to try so hard to outshine the other young women at court. She wouldn't have to worry constantly about losing her position.

She'd be able to outpace this gnawing shadow. It still feasted on her mind when she was alone, the Baptizer's command to repent echoing over and again in her head. But it would be different once she was Alexander's wife. There would be no more guilt. No more shame. Only love and respect and honor. He would give her that, all of that.

He would make her whole. Give her purpose. Give her a family.

"Finished, my lady."

"You look magnificent."

Magdalene smiled at her maids. "But not too magnificent?"

The girls shared a smile. "Of course you will not outshine the princesses," Rachel said.

Her sister, Rebecca, nodded. "Just come very close to it."

"Good." Today was to be Salome's shining moment. Her betrothed had come for Herod's birthday feast—the first Salome had actually met him. Their introduction had been cordial but cool.

Magdalene had made herself pay attention, hoping that her friend would be surprised by an instant affection, not unlike what she'd experienced with Alexander. But her future husband had scarcely paid the princess a moment's attention, and Salome had whispered her dismay at the thought of spending her life at the side of a man who didn't even look her way.

That would change today though. Today they would be presenting the dance that Salome had been working on for months. All the unmarried ladies of court would participate, but the princess would be the center of attention. She would showcase her agility and grace, her beauty, and what may be even more important—her desire to please her future husband.

Perhaps, if Magdalene was very careful, she'd be able to show the same thing to Alexander without taking any attention from Salome. A difficult balance to strike, but it could require as little as making eye contact during part of the dance.

"One last thing." Rachel crouched down to fasten on an anklet with bells. The other dancers would be wearing them too.

Magdalene nodded her approval. "Thank you. Enjoy your day, girls. I don't imagine I'll be back until dawn tomorrow."

The sisters' enthusiastic giggles followed her out into the corridor.

The festive atmosphere blanketed the palace, luring a smile onto Magdalene's lips even before she spotted Alexander in the crowd. She waved a good morning and tucked his handsome smile into her heart, but she hadn't the time to join him yet. She instead joined the group of young women around Salome.

The princess examined each of them closely. They'd been given matching clothing in white and gold, leaving her as the only figure in vibrant purple. Magdalene gave her a quick embrace when her inspection brought her near enough. "You look stunning!" she whispered in her ear.

Salome's cheeks flushed prettily. "Do you think so? I fear all Mother's ministrations won't be enough to actually earn my betrothed's regard."

"Nonsense. He will be smitten without question." She stepped back, arms held out. "Do I pass inspection?"

Salome chuckled. "Your clothing is perfect. Now if only you would put a veil over your face and perhaps chop off that hair, I may stand a chance of being prettier for a day."

"You outshine me from head to toe, Salome."

Salome shook her head, her smile sweet if amused. "An utter lie but one you may actually believe, so I thank you." She angled away. "We'll talk more later—I still haven't heard how your visit to Magdala with Alexander went last week."

They'd visited the villa twice already, but that particular trip had involved lingering in the town and visiting with all the neighbors—neighbors Alexander had charmed with ease, of course. Even Simon the Pharisee. And Simon had never done anything but scowl at Magdalene since Abba died and she attached herself to Herod's court. He made it glaringly clear what he thought of any Jewess who lived in the Roman fashion.

He might be right about some of his complaints, but that wasn't the point. The point was that he'd clearly recognized, just as Magdalene did, that Alexander could fix everything simply by being who he was.

None of which she had time to tell Salome now, so she simply said, "Yes. Later."

While her friend moved to the next young woman in their group, Magdalene searched the crowd for Joanna. As a married woman, she wouldn't be taking part in the dance, but she was never far from the action in the court, so she must be nearby. She finally spotted her with Khuza, reclining at one of the tables, talking to other guests with a bright smile. Magdalene made note of the table so she could find her later.

Her gaze swung past Archelaus too—he was watching her, his brows drawn. Magdalene lifted her chin and averted her face. He'd been doing that more and more lately, the more attention Alexander paid to her. It seemed he was one of those men who wanted only what he couldn't have.

Well. He'd had his chance, and he hadn't deemed her worth pursuing for more than an evening. He could regret that decision at his leisure now.

He won't regret it, something said inside her. *He'll be grateful. He knows the truth of what you are. How unworthy. How unlovable. He knows you're dirty. Filthy. Unclean.*

She spun away, tracing the henna pattern on her arm with a finger. Following its path, thinking of its design instead of the blood that had stained her skin in those same places. Pattern, not smears. Beauty, not tragedy.

Musicians took their places in the corner of the room, launching into a rousing song that soon had hands clapping and toes tapping. Magdalene let the rhythm seep into her mind, into her bones. She knew the plan was to let the musicians play for a few minutes to get the crowd in the right mood before Salome and the ladies took to the floor. She fell into line with the others, filing along to the side of the enormous chamber to await their cue.

The shadows at the edges of her vision pulsed in time to the beat. She let her eyes slide closed, not certain if it was to fend them off or embrace them. She loved music. Loved how it seemed to fill her limbs and spill out into a dance.

When it was time to take the floor with the others, she felt as though she were part of the music and it of her. She moved her arms and legs and hips exactly as the others were doing, careful to match them step for step, clap for clap, only ever pointing to Salome as where all eyes should be directed.

Except Alexander's. She certainly didn't mind that when the dance brought her whirling his way, his gaze was latched on her, not Salome, and he watched her with a small, warm smile. She caught his eye and tossed a smile at him too before she twirled away.

Her gaze clashed then with Archelaus's. He too was watching her, gaze heated but mouth absent a smile.

Her stomach tightened, and she nearly missed a step. But then the dance carried her away again and she pushed him from her mind. He was nothing. *You are nothing.* He was a mistake. *Your life is a mistake.* He wouldn't dare to interfere in her life once she and Alexander announced a betrothal. *You don't deserve Alexander.*

Her vision was more shadow than light as she spun to a halt in the line of women, her head light but her limbs heavy. A riot of applause only made the world contract still more, her senses swimming. She fought to focus. *Alexander. Focus on Alexander.*

Herod and his brother both stood, though Philip looked no more enthusiastic than he had thus far. Perhaps that was simply his way—Stoic, like a Roman, at least before the public. Perhaps he would be warmer, more effusive, in private. She hoped so, for Salome's sake.

Salome stood in the center of the room before the thrones, chest still heaving from exertion, cheeks flushed a lovely pink as she lifted her face toward her mother and the two tetrarchs.

Herod led the applause for another moment and then brought it to a slow halt by lifting his arms. "You have enchanted the whole assembly, Salome, and done honor to me on this special day. It is my great pleasure to offer you a favor. Whatever you choose, it shall be yours, up to half my kingdom."

Magdalene sucked in a surprised breath, along with the rest of the assembly. Many kings made a tradition of granting such favors during their birthday feasts, but Herod had always doled them out sparingly. The court alternately whispered that he was a miser...or wiser than most kings. Salome couldn't have anticipated the gift.

She recovered from her shock quickly though, dipping low. "You do me great honor, my lord. May I confer with my mother?"

Herod laughed. "Of course! And in the meantime—let the feasting begin!"

The music struck up again, loud and quick, making the shadows gather around Magdalene's vision once more. She exchanged an excited grin with Salome as her friend rushed by, on her way to Herodias's side.

Magdalene should go find a seat. Drink some water, perhaps eat something. That would make her feel better. She would seat herself at Alexander's side and enjoy the feast. She would...would...

Her feet didn't aim her toward Alexander though. Her mind spun, a too-familiar fog overtaking her. Was that Alexander coming to meet her? No. Archelaus. *Turn away. Run.* Instead, she felt her lips pull up, though she didn't tell them to. She watched her own arm lift in greeting. Her hips swayed more than she meant for them to.

A veil of shadow had fallen before her eyes, not quite as dark as the complete oblivion, but as if it were twilight rather than noonday. She could hear her own voice in her ears, feel the rumble of laughter in her throat and chest, but she may as well have been speaking another language for all she understood.

Familiar and strange, all at once. Wrong, unnatural…yet she knew she'd felt it before even if she never could have described it. And under it all, that throbbing ache.

Whatever she said, it brought a flash to Archelaus's eyes, a wicked little smile to his lips. He was close now, so close. He slid an arm around her—he must have, though she couldn't feel it. She couldn't hear what words fell from his lips. Then they were moving, and the veil darkened.

Is this what it's always like? How many times had she wondered that even as the darkness closed in? Would she awaken from this bout as she always did, a blank in her mind where memory should have been?

"Magdalene!"

The voice slashed through the veil, letting in a ribbon of light. Tangled, confused light that made her blink against it. Another face filled her vision. Familiar? Yes. There was hope attached to that face somewhere inside…somewhere…

Alexander. Of course! It was Alexander, and he looked furious as he shoved Archelaus away, saying something about taking his hands off her.

Yes. Yes, he shouldn't have his hands on her. She should have told him so. She blinked again, forcing another wisp of shadow away from her eyes. *Alexander.* She clung to the name in her mind, to the face before her, to all he represented.

The future. Hope. A life away from…*this.* No more shadows. No more emptiness. He would fill her. Fill her heart, her arms, her home, her womb. He'd give her a family. Make her matter again. He'd fix everything.

"…accost a maiden," he was saying, his face a thunderhead that sent its rage toward Archelaus.

Archelaus's laugh rang of mockery. "Maiden? You've clearly only known her a few days, stranger."

Alexander sneered. "I know all I need to. She is a young woman from the best of families, she exhibits moderation and modesty, she—"

Archelaus's bark of laughter cut him off. "Modesty! Moderation? Perhaps we're not speaking of the same girl. Mary of Magdala—Magdalene—this thing of beauty before us?" Archelaus cast a simmering look her way. "She certainly comes from a leading family, but she hasn't gained her position in Herod's court through either modesty or moderation, I assure you. Here is a woman who knows how to enjoy life to the fullest!" His arm came around her again, pulling her flush against him. "Isn't that right, my beauty?"

Enjoy life? She could only blink at him. She couldn't remember the last time she actually enjoyed life—likely before Abba died. Since then, every single thing had been in pursuit of making the pain retreat for one more hour, one more day. Trying to hold things together. Worrying, fearing, panicking, then pushing it all away with another chalice of wine, another morsel from a silver tray, another trip to the vomitorium to start it all over again.

Enjoy life—laughable.

Alexander's accusatory look had moved to her now, and it was scathing enough that she edged back a step, the veil going thinner again. "Magdalene? He is lying—right? You are not… you are not one of *these* women that the court is so full of. You're a good Jewish daughter of a good Jewish house."

"I…" Where now were those words that filled her mouth and dropped from her tongue like honey, without her command? Where were the pretty, beguiling smiles that sprang unbidden to her lips so often? She fumbled for them, groped about in her mind for what would make his expression melt back into affection, but she could find none.

Archelaus gaped at Alexander as if he'd taken leave of his senses. "You are aware that you met her here—in the court. Herod's court. Can you not take one look at her and see that she is not living the boring, modest life of a Jewess? Look at her hair, man, at her clothing!"

A flush stole over Alexander's cheeks. "Trappings. I don't mind the trappings—I've lived my life in Cyrene and Rome, after all, where Jews dress like the rest of the citizens more often than not. And I know she has been friends since childhood with Khuza's wife. That doesn't mean that she… Magdalene? Tell me it doesn't. Tell me it doesn't mean that you have sullied yourself as he's implying."

Sullied. Filthy. Unclean. She traced a finger over the henna pattern, longing for soap and water. "I…" She saw them all, the parade of men who had wooed her, had flattered her, had slipped gold bangles onto her wrists, hoops into her ears, necklaces around her neck. She remembered the men who had pressed her to a wall, kissed her.

What had she allowed? What had she given? She didn't even know. Too much of it was a blur of shadow and forgetfulness and pain.

She forced her hands to lift, to reach for him. "It doesn't matter. It will all be nothing. Our future will be bright, I'll give you all—"

"Will you?" Anger was muscling out the confusion on his face again, and he took a step away. "How can you, if you've given all to another already? I did not come here seeking a whore of Herod's court, Magdalene—I came looking for a chaste bride. *That* is what my father promised me—what yours promised him!"

The words slapped her, slashed, bit like a spear. She felt the pain in her stomach, so sudden it nearly doubled her over. "Please!" A gasp, that was all the word was. Begging. Imploring.

She reached out again, but he knocked her hand away. "What do you think I am? Do you hold me in such low esteem that you think I would degrade my family by taking a wife who had betrayed her heritage?"

No. No, he couldn't do this. He couldn't snatch all her hope away, replacing it with condemnation. "Alexander."

"Get away from me." Snarling now, he spun, strode away, and vanished into the crowd.

CHAPTER SIX

*N*o. She wanted to scream it, wanted to run after him, wanted to tell him whatever he needed to hear to stay with her, to give her a chance, to fix this mess she'd made of her life.

She made it a few steps before the weight of it hit her, sending her staggering.

He didn't *want* to fix her mess. He didn't want her as she was. He didn't want a woman who came to him with sin and stains and a history she couldn't even remember. He didn't want an imperfect bride.

He didn't want her. He'd only wanted the image his father, her father had painted of her. He wanted the illusion of who she'd once been. He had no interest in helping her become someone new now.

She made it out into the corridor before she fell to her knees. Pain radiated up her legs from where she connected with the unforgiving tiles, a perfect reflection of all she felt inside. Unforgiving, just like Alexander. Like all the world.

Pain—the pain provided a strange sort of solace. It faded, where the ache inside never had. It was there and gone, intense then just an echo. Easily controlled.

She pushed back to her feet before an approaching couple could reach her with their concern. No doubt they thought she'd tripped—or perhaps they thought she was drunk. Perhaps they, like everyone else, knew exactly what she was and hated her for it. Condemned her. Perhaps they saw her and screamed, "Unclean!" in their minds.

Perhaps they whispered it behind their hands as she ran by them. Perhaps that was what everyone back there said about her. Unclean, filthy, blemished, sullied.

Unworthy. Unworthy. Unworthy.

The words chased her down the hallway, out the door, up the stairs. She didn't even know where she was going, not really. Not until she saw the familiar rooftop sanctuary that Salome so loved, with its benches and cushions and tables, with its incomparable view of the landscape.

She stumbled to the half wall and braced her hands upon it. The stone was hot under her hands, uncomfortably so—a pain as welcome as the earlier one in her knees. Maybe it would purify her like fire.

Repent. That was what the Baptizer had said. *Purge me with hyssop, and I shall be clean: wash me, and I shall be whiter than snow.* The psalm filled her mind, a song as sweet as it was mysterious.

Hyssop could only cleanse the skin. It couldn't get at the stains within. Had she gone to the Jordan when John was there, he could have plunged her beneath the waters, but how could that have really changed anything? Nothing could ever make her clean again. She'd known that from the moment she scrubbed at the blood on her hands and sobbed at how it wouldn't come out. Sometimes she swore she could still see it in the cracks and crevices.

Repent. She squeezed her eyes shut. Abba had spoken of repentance once, when they asked him why he made sacrifices, why the Law told them to, why any of it mattered. *"Because,"* he had said, tweaking Azur's nose and then winking at Sarah and Magdalene in turn, *"the sacrifice is the expression of what our sins have cost us, the price we must pay. The sacrifice is a reminder that when we turn from those sins, when we truly repent of them, we do not just say we are sorry—we admit that our sin has come with a price and we seek not only forgiveness but a new understanding. We turn our bodies and our minds and our souls away from the sinful thing, toward God again."*

She hadn't understood his words then—she'd been only a child. Yet she could hear them so clearly now, when she hadn't thought of them for years. She remembered them, and they were one more bludgeon to her heart.

Sin had a cost—it always had a cost. That's what Abba had taught her. And she hadn't bulls or lambs or rams or pigeons enough nor silver enough to buy them, to atone for the sins she'd committed. The life of an animal could not restore the life she'd lost.

The pain of the hot stones had ebbed the longer she stood there. She lifted her hands, looked at her palms. They were red, but that was all. That would soon fade. She'd forget, as she forgot everything else, what it had even felt like.

And why? Why should she even bother trying to understand it anymore? Why continue the struggle? Her life was worthless—she'd bargained it away, exchanging all that really mattered for a few moments of oblivion.

Make it go away, she had begged over and over again. And it—whatever it was—had done just that. It had made it all go away—her value, her worth, her virtue, her heritage, her family. She'd lost everything. Everything. And she'd never get it back. No one that could give it would want to.

There was an answer though. She hitched up her stola and tunic enough that she could climb up onto the thick half wall. She'd sat there before with Salome, feeling perfectly secure with the wide stones bracing her.

She didn't want to feel safe today. What did safety matter? It was an illusion too, just like the Mary that Alexander had come here seeking. She stood, wobbling a bit in a gust of wind, moving forward until her toes dropped off the edge.

Jump. The voice jeered, challenged. *Jump and end it all. No one will miss you. The stain you'll leave on the earth below you now will be nothing compared to the stain your existence leaves behind you.*

She could. She could jump. End it. Magdalene held out her arms, let the wind whip around her. Would it tug her over the edge? She closed her eyes, tilting her face up to the hot midday sun.

What would come after, though? Abba had always spoken of the bosom of Abraham, where the faithful would be gathered. Heaven, the Baptizer had called it. But only the worthy went there.

She wasn't that. Which meant what? The vague Hades that the Gentiles spoke of? The flames of hell? Some of the Greeks in the court spoke of their souls bathing in the River Lethe, the waters of forgetfulness that removed all memory of their life on earth from their spirits.

A shudder overtook her. She had moments enough that she couldn't remember, moments that she knew were dark with sin. Forgetfulness had seemed a blessing when she begged for it, but now? No. An eternity of no memory was no eternity at all.

What then? Hell, with its flames and weeping and gnashing of teeth?

Tears stung her eyes. *I don't want to die.* Her arms shook. How could a thing be both the truth and yet so untrue? She didn't want to die—but she didn't want to go on living either, not like this. She wanted…she wanted…

Noise from below made her open her eyes. She looked down in time to spot two soldiers hurrying toward the palace from the prison, a basket in the arms of the first one.

She could have sworn she heard laughter in her ears, even though no one stood nearby. That, however, was what sent her scurrying down from the wall before the invisible someone could push her off.

"I don't want to die." She said the words out loud just to see how they tasted on her tongue. Bitter. They were only one more dilemma, not a solution.

Below, the soldiers called to one another, the gatekeepers granting entrance to the two newcomers, there "on Herod's orders."

What would Herod have ordered during his birthday feast?

Curiosity mixed with dread in her stomach as she made her way back down the stairs and into the throne room.

Horror threatened to swallow her whole. Magdalene raced from the throne room, from the palace, from the complex, her feet eating up the ground. Images raced even faster before her mind's eye—Salome, pale and wide-eyed and looking as though she'd lose her breakfast; Herodias, smug and pleased and with a dark spark glinting in her eyes; Herod, lips pressed tight together and regret in the lines of his face.

John the Baptizer, eyes vacant and staring out at them all from the severed head the soldier held up on a silver platter.

That was what Herodias had told sweet Salome to request. And Salome, ever obedient, had done it. Salome had whispered the words that Herod had to grant by his own dictate, and the result…death.

Always death. Everything came back to death, no matter how fast Magdalene ran away from it.

Soon her lungs burned, pain pierced her side, her sandals rubbed her ankles raw. Still, she would have kept going had a crowd of people not blocked her way.

Only when she paused, gasping for breath, did she hear Joanna calling from behind her, begging her to stop, to wait. Magdalene turned, finding her friend to be but a few steps away, also gasping for breath and holding a hand to the side that must be splitting.

"Where are you going?" Joanna wheezed between gulps of air, staggering to a halt beside Magdalene.

Where? That hadn't even mattered. "I don't know. Home? Away, mostly. I cannot…I cannot be there. Not now." Perhaps not ever. She squeezed her eyes shut, wishing it didn't mean that the images bludgeoned her anew. "They killed him. Just because he offended Herodias, they *killed* him!"

He'd been a good man. A righteous man. She'd known that after that one brief encounter. He had been a man who spoke the words of God. Didn't that by definition make him a prophet?

"He would have incited a rebellion," Herodias had said as she gloated over the horrific platter. "You did well, my husband, to first arrest him and now bring a halt to his treachery once and for all."

If Herod had replied, Magdalene hadn't heard it. She had been too busy elbowing her way past the swarms of acquaintances who didn't seem to understand that she had to escape right that moment.

Perhaps Joanna had understood though, to have kept pace with Magdalene this far. They'd reached the crossroads, a mile from Herod's palace. Usually here she would bear left, toward Magdala and then her villa, when there weren't crowds blocking the way.

Why were so many people about?

"I know. It was…" Joanna paused. "I can go months without being struck by how ruthless they can be, then something like this happens. And I think, 'I was not raised for this world.'

But where else can I go? Can we just hide away in your villa for the rest of time?" Her friend looked around with as much confusion as Magdalene felt. "What are all these people doing here?"

Magdalene shook her head and, experimentally, tried to straighten her torso. The stitch in her side still screamed, but it had eased enough for her to stand upright again. She cast her gaze over the crowd. Many of them she recognized—neighbors from Magdala or the surrounding region. But there were many unfamiliar faces too.

And there, one more than vaguely known. "Barnabas? Barnabas!"

Her steward moved with a group a stone's throw away, though his head swung around upon hearing his name. It took him a long moment to locate her, though his eyes lit when he did. "My lady!" he shouted, waving an arm. "Have you come to hear the Rabbi?"

Rabbi? Was that what all these people were here for? How odd. Magdalene sucked in another long breath and picked her way through the crowd. It required moving with them along the road, but it wasn't as though she had any burning desire to get to the villa, and this direction would get her away from the palace as much as the other would.

When she was close enough that she didn't have to shout, she said, "What rabbi? I was on my way home."

Barnabas's eyes danced. Had they always been so merry, so…bright? They struck a stark contrast to the ones she'd seen so recently, sparking with darker glee. "His name is Jesus, from the Nazareth region, I believe. From what I've heard, He preaches much like John called the Baptizer."

The name struck an arrow through her heart. "Does He?"

Joanna's hand gripped her arm. "We might as well go along. Hear Him."

No! The scream sounded so loud in her ears that she had to brace her head between her hands. The darkness closed in, heavy and fast and suffocating.

Hands pulled her back—Joanna's, Barnabas's.

"We should definitely take you to the Rabbi," Barnabas said. "I have heard He is a mighty healer."

"I don't need a healer." Even as she said the words, she could hear the strain in her voice, the pain.

Joanna moved closer, looking intently at her. "Perhaps you do—all those times you say you cannot remember, that things go black…perhaps it is a strange headache. Perhaps this Rabbi can cure you of it."

Magdalene shook her head, the thing that so often seized her limbs making her pull away, that refusal still screaming inside her.

Joanna gripped her arm all the tighter, concern slamming onto her face. "Magdalene, what's the matter? Do you need me to go back for Alexander?"

A sob tore through her, loosening the grip of the shadows on her limbs but not dislodging her two companions at all. She shook her head again. "He wants nothing to do with me. He… he…I am not…"

Barnabas still frowned, but Joanna's eyes lit with understanding. She linked their arms together. "Come. We need something to take our minds off the court and all it represents. An afternoon in the countryside, listening to a new teacher, will be just the thing."

Would it? She couldn't think that it would help a bit, but at the moment, doing the opposite of what she'd normally have done seemed like just the thing. Though it took gritting her teeth and felt like she was wading through water, she forced her legs to move along with Joanna and Barnabas.

They were three of hundreds who gathered at the base of a small knoll and settled into the grass. Barnabas knew everyone there, it seemed, and somehow used his greetings of one person after another to advance them through the crowd, until they were within the first few rows of people.

The grass was cool and scratchy under her, and as she looked out over the crowd, she became keenly aware of how odd she and Joanna were—the only two women dressed in the Roman fashion, though many other women were present, all with their heads covered. The men represented more of a variety, from Jews of various stations to soldiers to a few that she guessed to be wealthy merchants.

Most paid her no attention, but a few looked their way—some with curiosity, others with outright scorn. She recognized one of them as Simon the Pharisee. No surprise there. He was always wherever people were gathered and very seldom smiling about it.

Just to escape his glower, she turned her face forward, toward the knoll. A knot of men stood there, conversing among themselves. Which one was the Teacher? The tallest? Or perhaps that one who had a slender, scholarly look about him?

It was neither of those who stepped forward and held out His arms. The crowd fell into silence at His movement, though Magdalene couldn't be sure why, not at first. He didn't look like anyone remarkable. He wore a dusty tunic and a frayed belt. His hair was windblown. Then He smiled, and she understood. Something small and bruised within her quieted, and she leaned forward, too eager to hear what He'd say.

"What is the kingdom of heaven?" The Rabbi, Jesus, looked out over the crowd and motioned past them, back toward the palace a mile off. "We know the kingdoms of earth. We have learned the histories of Judah and Israel, of Greece and Rome. We know how rulers rise and fall, power waxes and wanes. We know that those with crowns upon their heads think they have the power of life and…death."

His gaze flicked down, skirting over them.

Did He know? Did He know they'd come from the palace? Did He know what had just happened there?

He couldn't have, not so soon after the beheading. Could He? Perhaps John's disciples had been outside the prison when it happened. Perhaps they'd heard the command or seen that wretched basket or even glimpsed the execution. Perhaps, if this Jesus was truly a friend of John's, they'd already rushed to tell Him.

"But I tell you no king of this earth has power except that God has given it to him. Seeking after these earthly kingdoms will give you nothing—but repent, I say, and seek after the kingdom of heaven! For it is like a pearl of great price. What man, when he finds such a pearl, will not sell all he has to acquire it? And what man, if he digs in a field and finds a treasure buried there, will not sell all he has and buy the field for the treasure it holds?"

Her eyes stung. All she worked for, all she'd traded so much for—was it worthless, then, compared to heaven? Is that what He meant? What would He have her do, give it all up?

For what? Or how? How did one grasp heaven in one's hand like a pearl or a buried treasure?

The Rabbi paused, looking out over the group. A smile played over His mouth again. "Or perhaps you wonder at this parable. How, you may say, can a man hold heaven in his hand? How can he win a kingdom like this, that cannot be won with horses and chariots and military might? Amen, friends, I say to you that heaven will not be inherited by the princes of this world, but by the poor in spirit. By those who are persecuted for the sake of righteousness. You want a great reward in heaven? Then show mercy. Be pure in heart. Hunger and thirst not after bread and wine, but after goodness and justice."

Goodness and justice. Poverty of spirit. Righteousness. Purity.

Unclean! Filthy, soiled, sullied. Impure. Impure!

Tears wet her cheeks and shook her shoulders. It was true, all those things that screamed inside her head. She was all of that and more—worse. She was a wretch. A sinner. Unworthy of the call to heaven.

But she wanted it. Oh, how she yearned for goodness and justice and righteousness. For purity, if ever someone like her could regain it.

What hope was there of that though? She'd seen it clearly in Alexander's eyes—she was worthless. Worthless and unworthy, and this Teacher would see it the moment He looked at her, just as everyone else did. He would look at her with the same eyes that John had, and He would *know*. He would know she was a sinner. He would know what shadows feasted on her soul. He would see and He would judge, and He would be right.

His gaze meandered now instead of sweeping, catching on people here and there. Magdalene's fingers fisted in her stola. Maybe He would look at her. She hoped He would—no, she feared He would. His gaze would surely rip her to shreds.

Then it happened. His eyes moved again, and they came to a rest on her. She felt the power of it all the way to her core, just as she had when John looked at her, but even more so. And yet…different. So different.

Men looked at her all the time. With lust, with longing, with admiration, with calculation. Others with judgment and dismissal.

But this Jesus—He looked at her with…she hadn't even a word for it. Compassion? Understanding?

That couldn't be, could it?

Then His gaze moved on, and she was left gasping for breath. More, she needed more! She needed everything. Instruction, learning, direction. She needed to know what to do to find this heaven of which He spoke. She needed to know how to become the things that were worthy of it.

He lifted His arms again. "Whoever is sick among you, come. Be healed."

Healed. Yes! *That* was what she needed most, to be healed of this thing eating her up inside. Magdalene surged to her feet, beating back the part of her that told her to turn and run away instead, that hissed and groaned, that said it was better to wallow in what she knew than to risk it all on a promise that must be empty.

The desperation of her soul won out over the fear and shadows. Praying she didn't step on anyone or cut off someone even more desperate than she, she stumbled her way forward, past the front row of seated people, into the space before the Rabbi.

For a moment, she stood there alone before the eyes of the hundreds of people gathered on the hillside. For a moment, the worry of what they must be thinking stabbed her, fear clawed its way up her spine.

Then Jesus looked at her again. Thoughts of anyone else, everyone else, fled.

He had the answers—He had *all* the answers. She could see them there in His eyes, and from somewhere inside came a scream she could scarcely comprehend. She knew Him—or something did. Something dark and hate-filled and empty. That something knew Him and recoiled and tried to take control of her arms and legs and send her away.

No! She wouldn't let it happen, not this time. To keep it from winning, she fell to her knees before the Teacher, reaching toward Him. Her fingers stopped just shy of the toes peeking out of His sandals. "Please! Rabboni!" They were the only words she could force from her lips.

Jesus knelt beside her and rested a hand on the top of her head. His hand was warm as sun-parched stone but not heavy. Light. For a long moment, He stayed just like that, while the darkness thrashed and writhed inside her, trying to escape Him.

"Be still. Leave her." He didn't shout the words, but they echoed through her being, into every corner and crevice.

She jolted, the shadows screaming and bunching up, ready to fight—but then He whispered something else, something she didn't hear over the cries, and then…then…stillness. Light. Peace.

The sobs that shook her now were like fresh springs in the desert, cleansing. "Thank You. Thank You."

He withdrew His hand. "You are healed, daughter."

Healed. Daughter.

He wasn't old enough to be her father, was scarcely older than her at all—but that word was the sweetest of any He could have chosen. It spoke of the thing she most missed, the relationship that had been stolen from her by violence. *Abba.* She missed him every day. She missed him from the depths of her soul. His death had taken more than just his presence from her life. It had taken her hope and her identity.

But that one word, spoken from the lips of Jesus, restored it all somehow. That word told her that she still had a father, even if he wasn't with her on earth. She was still beloved. She was still worthy to be cared for and protected. She was still worth fighting for.

The fight inside her, though, had stopped. Those shadows that had pummeled their way into her life were gone. Her hands and feet and arms and legs were her own. Her mouth would never again say words she didn't tell it to. She had been restored. Renewed. Reborn.

All thanks to the gentle authority of the Rabbi called Jesus.

Magdalene couldn't have said how long she stayed just as she'd been, prostrate on the ground. She wept until her tears ran dry, and then she concentrated on breathing until the gasps calmed and her breaths regulated. Vaguely she was aware of Jesus moving down the line of supplicants, murmuring words she couldn't quite hear.

Eventually she sat up, wiping her face with the hem of her stola and not caring a whit about the cosmetics that transferred to the cloth. A glance around showed her that most of the crowd had dispersed, and the sun had somehow gone from overhead to nearing the horizon.

Joanna and Barnabas flanked her. Her friend sat with eyes closed and face lifted to the sky, humming psalms that Magdalene hadn't heard her sing since she moved to the palace complex after her marriage. Her arms were bent at the elbow, palms open as if to receive manna from heaven.

Barnabas sang to Joanna's humming, a sweet, pitch-perfect tenor that resonated deep inside Magdalene's soul. He too had his eyes closed, face and palms lifted to the sky.

What was this feeling that rested upon them? No, *feeling* wasn't the right word, it was more than that. Deeper than that, not as fleeting as a feeling. A feeling was just a note, but this was resonance, harmony, echoes.

She should probably stand. Recommend they return to the villa. They should eat, rest, talk about what happened here today.

Instead, she closed her eyes, held tilted palms and face upward, and sang along with her friends.

CHAPTER SEVEN

FRIDAY

The closer they drew to Golgotha, the thinner the crowd became. Finally, Magdalene spotted a familiar face, one that surely unleashed a torrent of relief in the heart of the other Mary. "John!" She lifted her free arm and waved it.

The youngest of the Twelve spun, spotted them, and ran toward them, pulling his mother to his chest as soon as he was near enough. She clung to him with a sob. "My son! Where is your brother?"

John shook his head. "I do not know where any of the others are. I trailed Peter to the trial, but by the time the rooster crowed, he had vanished from my sight. I don't know where they went—I knew only that I must do what I have always done and follow the Lord."

Magdalene shuddered against a cool breeze that whipped up the hill. She had thought the Twelve so strong, so capable. They had healed in the Lord's name, they had done great works too, and they always received more teaching than the rest of them, even those who had followed Him faithfully these three years. They were something special, she'd thought.

But like sheep, they had scattered the moment they lost sight of their Shepherd.

"They are afraid, they must be." The other Mary rubbed a hand over her son's back and pulled away again. "If I were one of you men, I would be too. I cannot think they'll arrest us women, but the rest of you surely have targets upon your backs."

Fierce anger pierced Magdalene's chest, so sharp she didn't know from where the arrow of it came or even where it was directed. At the Twelve, for abandoning Him now? Judas, for putting Him in the situation? Jesus Himself, for insisting they come to Jerusalem for this Passover, even though they had all warned Him that it was too dangerous?

Yes, but no. In that moment, she had anger enough to direct at the whole world, it seemed. But mostly, it was aimed squarely at herself. She should have insisted. She should have stopped Judas somehow. She should have been there last night.

No, more than that. She should have never given the religious leaders cause to complain against Him. She was a stain on His reputation, bringing Him down by mere association with her. Her mistakes, her sins, her poor decisions had led to this.

She might as well be the one reaching now for the hammer.

⁕⁕⁕

THREE YEARS EARLIER

Mornings at the villa always dawned more tranquilly than mornings at the palace, but not since her father was alive and her family surrounded her had Magdalene opened her eyes to such peace. It took her a long moment to even identify what that strange, soft, bubbling sensation was in her chest.

Joy. That was it. Something she hadn't known in years. Something she'd thought she'd never know again.

She stretched, letting it bubble all the way to the tips of her fingers and toes, to suffuse every bit of her. Even letting a smile turn her lips.

Arguably, her life was still a shambles—Alexander wouldn't forgive her just because Jesus had healed her, she had probably offended Herodias by flying from the court as she'd done, and though she could never imagine returning to that life of sin, that decision didn't erase the consequences of the ones already committed.

And yet even that couldn't cast a shadow over the day, because the shadows themselves were gone from her soul.

She rose from her bed, washed her face, dressed for the day, and then moved to the window to look out over her estate. This had always been her favorite place in the world, even more than the larger holdings Azur had inherited outside Jerusalem. The way the vines twisted and grew, the lush leaves that sheltered the plump grapes beneath them; the olive orchard stretching upward in the distance.

Had she even appreciated the beauty of this place since Abba died? No. All she'd seen was the responsibility. She'd feared that she would fail, that no one would listen to or respect her authority here because she was a woman, that she would lose everything.

What a fool she'd been, to think any of this was really hers to begin with. Would the vines care if she died? Had they mourned her father? No. Would the olive trees weep if she moved away? Of course not. Would the land revolt if she didn't keep an iron fist on the legers? Laughable.

This villa didn't truly belong to her any more than Israel belonged to Caesar. Perhaps the law of man said it was so—but the earth and all that was in it belonged to God. All she and her family had been given was truly His. They were but His stewards. And just as she could trust or remove Barnabas, God could trust or remove *them*.

Strange how that brought peace this morning instead of anxiety. She would do her best to take care of this land, this place, these people. But she would also be sure to remember from now on that neither their labor nor its fruits nor the soil in which it was rooted was ever truly hers. She had no power but that which God gave her, as Jesus had said yesterday.

For the first time in years, her heart yearned toward prayer. Psalms she'd thought she'd forgotten clamored for a place in her mind and on her tongue, and she smiled as she selected one to sing. It kept her company as she walked the perimeter of the house and then went in search of Joanna.

Her friend lounged on a chaise on the east-facing side of the house, a cup of steaming chamomile in hand. She greeted Magdalene with a smile. "I didn't think I would ever see that Magdalene again in the morning. You look…like the girl you used to be."

"Better. That girl had never seen the shadows to know how much she should appreciate the light." The steaming pot sat nearby, along with a second cup, so she poured herself some too and added a dollop of honey from the bowl of it at hand.

Even that fragrance seemed more poignant this morning, more real, more vibrant. She lowered herself to the end of Joanna's chaise and looked toward the rising sun too. "It feels… it feels as though my soul is rising up to meet the Lord like the sun, after a very long, dark night."

Joanna touched an encouraging hand to her elbow. "I didn't realize how sick you were. Not until Jesus approached you. You were thrashing about like—"

"Like it wasn't me?" It wasn't. How many times had she very nearly grasped that and yet not been able to put words to it? Even now, the only words that could possibly explain it seemed too terrifying, too strange. "Do you think it was… demons?"

Joanna shuddered. "I don't know. I never would have said so. And yet—He told something to leave you."

"And it—or even they?—did." Magdalene nodded and faced her friend so that Joanna could see clearly that she wasn't going to shrug away from the truth. Not anymore. "That must have been it. I must have invited them in when I was in the throes of grief, begging someone, anyone to make it go away."

Those had been her words, screamed into the night. *Make it go away! Make me forget!* Something had agreed, and had done just that.

If she had known the cost, the chains it would put her in… but she knew now. She was free now. She would never again let anyone or anything possess her soul. She took a sip of her tea and tried to look into the future, even by a day.

It stretched blank and empty before her though. Gleaming with hope, yes. But she had to fill it with something. And she must choose carefully what that something would be. "Is Jesus teaching anywhere else in the region? He can't have left yet, can He? I need to learn more."

Joanna smiled. "Barnabas came out minutes before you found me—he was looking for you but had missed you. He was going into Magdala to learn what he could."

Then learn it he would. Magdalene breathed a bit easier with that promise. "Good. Even if I have to follow Him to the next town, I must know more. I must hear more of His teachings."

"I was thinking the same." Joanna ran a finger around the rim of her cup, looking into it but clearly seeing something more. "I'll have to speak with Khuza first, of course."

"Of course." Joanna's husband was no tyrant, to be sure, but he was still something to tie her here, to Herod's palace. She couldn't just go wandering about the countryside with the Rabbi.

Magdalene could though. The thought sent a thrill through her. She had nothing at all keeping her tied down to one place. No husband, no children, and the villa didn't need her to be here. She was free to learn at the feet at Jesus. She could go wherever He went next, spend a few weeks or even months listening to His teachings, if she was brave enough.

Never in her life had she been somewhere without at least one trusted friend or family member though. Her father, her siblings, Joanna. Someone had always been by her side. Would she really go anywhere if her friend couldn't go with her?

A maidservant came out with a tray of food, offering them a small smile that Magdalene returned wholeheartedly. The bread! It smelled amazing, and her mouth watered even looking at the slices of cheese and fruit. She filled a plate, they blessed the food, and each bite was an explosion of flavor upon her tongue.

It was as though she hadn't truly tasted anything in years, if ever she had at all. She savored each bite with a sigh as her mind pondered the question of what she would do.

When it came to exact answers, she didn't have them. She only knew that she needed more of the Rabbi's teachings than she'd gotten yesterday.

Barnabas returned a few minutes later, excitement in his eyes. "Ah, mistress! I was seeking news of the Teacher."

"Yes, good." She scooted forward, to the edge of the chaise. "Will He be in the area for long?"

"A few more days, at least. He is dining today at the home of Simon the Pharisee."

That made sense—Simon had one of the largest homes in town, and he always hosted teachers and scribes when they traveled through the area, so that the public could gather in the room and even outside on the streets to hear what they had to say. Abba had hosted several such feasts here too, but it was less convenient for the townsfolk, given that they were out-side the village.

She nodded. "Wonderful. We should all go to hear Him. And if you think He and His companions would be interested in joining us here before they leave, please do extend that invi-tation as well."

Surprise and delight lit dual flames in his eyes. "Of course, my lady. I would be pleased to extend the invitation and announce it in town if He accepts."

She hadn't issued any such invitations to traveling teachers since Abba's death—she had been too busy forgetting, and with ingratiating herself with Herod's court. Regret for that heated her cheeks. "I am sorry. I have made us neglect our responsibilities to our neighbors."

The kindness in his smile was completely undeserved, and all the more precious for that. "Your father's death was a terrible blow. I am only glad to see life in your eyes again, mistress."

"Well." She drained the last of the chamomile from her cup. "We have hours yet before Simon's feast will begin. This morning, would you have time to go over the accounts with me, Barnabas? I'd like to see what we could spare to support the Teacher's travels."

Barnabas's smile answered even before his words. "Of course I have time. And you can be as generous as you like— the vineyards and orchard have been flourishing."

Simon's house was impossible to miss. It dominated the main thoroughfare through Magdala, standing proud and tall among its humbler neighbors. By the time Magdalene, Joanna, and Barnabas approached the home, a crowd had already gathered in the streets, clustering around the windows and door so they would be able to hear the Teacher.

"We should have come earlier," Magdalene murmured to her companions, clutching the alabaster jar she carried against her side. It had the costliest of her perfumes inside, worth more silver than what she otherwise had on hand. All her jewelry was still at the palace—but this was good as gold. She would give it to the Rabbi or to His disciples, and they could sell it and live on the money for months.

Barnabas chuckled. "There will be room for us inside, my lady."

"Oh." Of course. She'd forgotten that the space inside was always reserved for the more prestigious visitors and guests. Honestly, she'd gone to only one or two such gatherings. She'd been too young, and then too uninterested, and then too... overcome.

It seemed wise to let Barnabas lead the way through the throng, into the door, and to wherever in the main gathering room he thought they belonged. They weren't invited guests, so obviously they wouldn't sit at the table, but he had soon found them positions against the wall with an excellent view of the head, where Jesus would surely be positioned, and with a bench behind them if they grew weary of standing.

Magdalene drew in a long breath and shifted from foot to foot, looking around for a glimpse of the Teacher. Neither He nor any of the men who'd been with Him yesterday—His disciples?—were within view, but their host soon entered the room, laughing with another of the leading men of the area. Jonas, wasn't it? He was a Pharisee too, if she recalled correctly.

They spotted her and sneered.

Oh no—she hadn't thought to change from her Roman-styled clothing or add a head covering, so busy had she been in choosing what gift to give the Teacher! No wonder they looked at her like that. How disrespectful she must seem, showing up in Simon's home with her hair only bound by a braid, not covered.

What should she do? Rush home? But then she'd miss much of the conversation, and that was her whole purpose in coming, not to impress Simon or Jonas. She couldn't leave before Jesus even came.

For now, she simply lowered her eyes and slid a bit more behind Barnabas, keeping her alabaster flask hidden in the folds of her stola. If she had a chance afterward, she would apologize to Simon for her oversight. She would assure him that she'd changed and would be leading a more modest life from now on. And then she'd prove it day by day.

A commotion at the front told her that the guest of honor had arrived, and her pulse galloped in response. The neighbors gathered in the streets greeted Him with shouts, and she heard several pleas for a touch, for healing.

"I brought my brother, Teacher!"

"Master, my mother—please, heal my mother."

Whether He responded with words or not she couldn't have said, but He must have responded with actions, because as many requests as there had been, there were then as many cries of gratitude and surprise.

Her heart felt like it might burst from her chest. Who was this man, that He could heal so many, so effortlessly? A touch, a word, and ailments fled. *Demons* fled. When had such a thing happened since the age of the prophets?

She glanced at Joanna, Barnabas, the others around them. Her friends wore expressions every bit as excited as her own must be, but the same could not be said of everyone. Several frowned or looked confused. Others seemed irritated and shifted from foot to foot, clearly impatient.

Simon had his arms crossed over his chest and stared at the door with pursed lips. He exchanged a few words with another of the men standing nearby, who looked just as dour. Were they annoyed that Jesus was engaging with the common people outside rather than rushing in? Couldn't they see that His compassion was part of what made Him so remarkable?

Apparently not. When Jesus finally entered, three companions with Him, Simon actually waved away the servant who had come forward with a bowl of water and a towel to wash their feet. Magdalene pressed her lips tight at the insult. Guests were *always* offered this basic hospitality, not just to show them respect but to wash the dust of the road from their feet before they sat on one's cushions. Why would he do such a thing?

He must want to insult the Teacher. There was no other explanation, and it made her pulse thud in a whole new way. To invite Him only to snub Him was unspeakably rude. But Simon whispered to a few of his friends, pointed around the table, and they all moved to the positions closest to the head where he would sit.

Only then did he turn to Jesus. "Welcome, Rabbi." He spoke with a grand gesture, motioning to the table—the *foot* of the table. But he didn't approach Him as he should have, offering no kiss of greeting, not even a Roman-style clasp of the wrist. "Please, make yourselves comfortable. These are your…friends?"

Jesus's smile didn't waver. He moved, not to the seat halfway up the table that remained unclaimed by the others, but to the foot, the position farthest from the host, the lowliest. "Thank you, friend. These are three of My disciples, yes— Peter, James, and John. The others are traveling throughout the country at the moment, preaching and healing the sick."

Simon snorted his opinion of that. "Of course. Your *disciples* are no doubt doing as much good as You Yourself have done in our town." He said *disciple* as though it was a mockery instead of evidence that this Teacher had lessons so worth learning that men would dedicate months of their lives to following Him and studying at His side.

Worse, Simon delivered the whole sentence as though Jesus had in fact been doing harm instead of good.

He strode to the head of the table and took his seat, signaling that all the other guests should do the same. Jesus and His three disciples did as well, though where the other guests folded their feet under them without compunction, they kept their own awkwardly off the cushions, clearly not wanting to soil them with dust from the road.

Indignation burned in Magdalene's chest. Not only was Simon's behavior a snub, it was a snub that would cause these men discomfort through the whole meal. Simon had proclaimed not just to Jesus but to everyone in attendance that he considered the Rabbi a mockery.

He wasn't that though, she knew it to her marrow, to her very soul. He was at the least a rabbi, but He must indeed be more—He must be a prophet, to be able to heal people, to have authority over demons.

A prophet. Here, among them. In the same house. A prophet who had power enough not only to heal but to send His disciples out to do the same.

How was that possible? When had it ever been done? There had been a school of prophets in the days of Elisha, yes, but the stories of them didn't include miracles like this. Even Moses had never been able to confer his anointing onto another in such a way.

A shiver danced up her spine. From where she stood, she could see Jesus in profile—the faint smile lines around His eyes, the way His cheeks rose toward them when He smiled, the unassuming confidence with which He sat.

Magdalene gripped her jar tighter. In the last three years, she'd met so many men. Ambitious men, selfish men, arrogant men, powerful men, wealthy men. Every time, she'd evaluated them just as they did her—how good-looking they were, how rich, what she could get from them, what they would expect of her.

She was accustomed to men who wore the finest linen and silk, who drank from silver and gold, who played with the future of empires. Yet here sat this man from Nazareth, with calluses on His hands, skin bronzed from the sun, and something about Him that said He ranked higher than them all.

He had looked at her yesterday, and no lust had flashed through His eyes. He had touched her, and instead of taking, He had given something miraculous. He had asked nothing in return.

He was what these others only pretended to be, and she knew it because the very darkness that had taken possession of her had told her so. It had recognized Him. It had cried out against Him.

That darkness had never recoiled in fear of Herod or Archelaus or Alexander. That darkness hadn't reacted so strongly even to John the Baptizer, though he was clearly of God too. Only this man, this Jesus, had made the demons tremble and flee.

Tears gathered behind her eyes just as they had yesterday, a torrent of gratitude and wonder. She didn't deserve His compassion, His healing. She didn't deserve the second chance that He'd given her. Yet He'd offered it anyway.

The men at the table were talking, but she couldn't hear them above the rushing in her ears, and she'd never be able to control the sobs knotting up in her chest. She needed to escape this room before she embarrassed not only herself but Barnabas. Not daring to try even to whisper an excuse to her friends lest she lose control, she simply gave Joanna's wrist a squeeze and then slipped away from the wall.

Her goal was to keep her head tucked down, to weave behind the other guests, and to escape through the front door without anyone noticing her. She would wait outside for the meal to end and press her gift into the Rabbi's hands then. It seemed a fine goal, except that she couldn't resist one more glance at Jesus.

He glanced up at the same time, and His gaze landed on her. Did He recognize her from yesterday? Was that why He smiled?

It was her own heart that overwhelmed her better sense this time, not some shadowy puppeteer. Despite her plans to avoid all notice, she couldn't simply leave—not when He'd seen her, not when the enormity of what He'd done for her rose before her again, not when she saw Him there, at the last seat when He should have been in the first, dust and dirt still clinging to the sandals that Simon wasn't even fit to untie.

Those words—John's words, as he spoke about the One to come. This man?

This man.

She knew it as she ignored the gasps of the surprised guests and moved toward the table. She knew it as she knelt beside the dusty feet of the Rabbi. She knew it as she let the cleansing rain of tears fall onto His soiled toes. She had tears enough to wet His feet, but the only thing at hand to dry them was the hem of her garment, and she couldn't exactly lift that.

Then her braid fell over her shoulder in a thick mass. Her hair, her crowning glory. A sign of her beauty, a sign of her shame. What better to use to remove the filth from His feet, just as He'd removed it from her soul?

She untied the bottom and used the locks as a towel, crying and wiping until the dust of travel had been removed and her gratitude left her exhausted, kneeling there before Him. She kissed one foot and then the other, but even that wasn't enough. He deserved more than tears and hair. He deserved more even than a servant with a bowl of water. He deserved the treatment given kings.

The flask. She took out the stopper, lifted it, and poured the precious oil over His feet. The sweet aroma wafted upward like a prayer. She rubbed it in, kissing His feet again and again to seal her gratitude into Him.

The room had fallen silent. It bludgeoned her now, weighed upon her, threatened to suffocate her. When she lifted her head, they would all be staring. They would all be judging her. They would call her mad.

She didn't care. This Teacher, this Prophet was worthy of all humility. She would abase herself, embarrass herself all over again if it restored to Him even a bit of the honor Simon had refused Him. She would pour out every last drop of perfume. She would give Him every ounce of silver and gold. He deserved it.

"Have you something to say, Simon?"

Jesus's voice swept over her, somehow comforting even though it carried a note of challenge.

Another beat of silence, and then Simon said, "I? No, Teacher. What could I possibly have to say?"

The Rabbi hummed, and it sounded both amused and disbelieving. "Well, I have something to say to you."

Though she didn't look up, she could tell from the sounds of shifting bodies that Simon and the other men had all straightened. "Have You? Go ahead, then. Tell me."

Magdalene kept her head bowed over Jesus's feet, her hands wrapped around His ankles, the scent of the perfume so strong it made her light-headed. She had no desire to move though. Not until He told her to.

"There were two people who both owed money to a banker. One owed five hundred denarii, and the other owed fifty. Neither of them had the money to pay this banker back. Now, suppose the banker forgave both debts—wiped them from his record books and said neither ever had to pay him even a single denarius. Who do you think would love the banker more?"

Simon cleared his threat. "I think it would be the man who was forgiven the larger debt."

"You're right about that." Jesus leaned down, took Magdalene by the shoulder, and raised her up until she was sitting on her heels. His face—it wasn't as handsome as Alexander's or Archelaus's. It hadn't the refinement of Herod's. But it was surely the most beautiful face she'd ever seen as He looked at her in the way Abba always had, but even more. Absent any frustration, any hint that she didn't measure up to His expectations.

He touched a finger to her chin. "Do you see this woman?" Perhaps the words were aimed at Simon, but His gaze stayed on her. "When I entered your house, Simon, you gave Me no water for My feet—but this woman has washed My feet with her tears and dried them with her hair. You gave Me no kiss of greeting, but she has not ceased kissing My feet. You gave Me no oil for My head, but she poured perfume on My feet."

Magdalene swallowed past the dryness of her throat. Clearly no one else understood what she was doing, but He did. He knew. He knew that her heart was simply overflowing.

Though His finger fell away, His gaze did not. "I know what you were thinking—that she is a woman of many sins. And so she was. But those great sins you so long to name are forgiven, and the forgiveness of it spurred this outpouring of love. Abundant love for the abundant forgiveness. Far more than those would offer who are only forgiven a little."

Even had it been appropriate for her to speak, she couldn't have. Her throat was clogged with new gratitude. He had spoken already of healing, He had called her "daughter." But dare she really hope that her sins had been wiped clean?

The corners of His lips turned up. "Yes, Mary. Your sins are forgiven."

From all around the table, Simon's friends broke into grumbling, murmuring. "Who is this man to forgive sins?"

"What authority could He possibly have to declare such a thing? Only God can forgive!"

"Blasphemy!"

Magdalene ignored them all. "You know my name?"

The Master's smile grew. "Mary of Magdala, the whole world will know your name. What you did for Me here today will never be forgotten."

For three long years, darkness had filled her. Now the light felt as though it would burst through each pore—not because she wanted any fame. Not because of what she had done at all, but because if anyone ever spoke about it, it would be because of *Him*. Because they would seek to honor Him and look to any example already set.

The Pharisees' questions reverberated through her mind—*"Who is this man to forgive sins?"*

She didn't have the answer, not exactly. But she would spend the rest of her life finding out, if He let her.

CHAPTER EIGHT

FRIDAY

Hammer blows rang out, each one making them all jump even more than the screams of the three men being executed at the top of the hill. Magdalene could feel each metal blow down to her marrow, and she was only one of Jesus's friends. What must it be like for His mother, who had carried Him in her womb against all odds? Who had cared for Him and tended Him? She who had watched Him grow into this man who had changed everything?

Everything.

Another metallic *clang*, another wince. They were not her hands being pierced, not her feet. Not her heart in quite the same way as Imma Mary's would be pierced. But the pain nearly undid her regardless. Magdalene felt as though she was standing again on the precipice of the palace roof, looking out over the promise of oblivion below.

Death had seemed a friend that day, but praise God that He had stopped her before she plummeted to meet it. Had she stood before the Righteous Judge back then, He would have declared her guilty without question.

She'd deserved death. Deserved condemnation. If she were to believe the Pharisees, she deserved it still, because the forgiveness Jesus offered was powerless. If she were to believe the Sadducees, then even if she *was* forgiven, it would mean only eternal sleep after the moment of death, no Paradise where someday body and soul would be reunited in joy.

Jesus had promised her more though. He had promised her that if she followed Him, He would lead her to life everlasting. To heaven. To God Himself.

John tried to move between them and the scene, spreading his arms wide. "You don't need to watch this. I can take you to safety if—"

"No." Imma Mary didn't shake her head, didn't push him away. She also left no room for argument in her voice. "I will not leave Him."

"Nor I."

"Nor I." Magdalene hated the quaver in her voice, but it was no sort of indecision that shook her. It was the fact that the cries from the three men turned to strangled, weak sounds as soldiers raised the crosses into their prepared holes.

He was there, in the center. Her Lord. Her Master. Her Savior. The Christ. He was there with agony upon His face.

Oh, my Jesus! She wanted to scream it, but a sob tangled with the words in her throat. *"Don't weep for Me,"* He'd just commanded them. But how could she not? This wasn't fair. He had done nothing wrong, nothing but challenge the authority of the priests and scribes. He had done nothing deserving of death at the hands of the Romans.

She was the one whose sins should have put her in the path of justice. Not Jesus.

She pushed past John, her gaze on that center cross. She must get closer. She must remain at His feet as she promised she would. His mother kept pace with her, both of them ignoring John's cry that they stay back, which of course meant that he and his mother surged to keep up with them instead.

The soldiers stopped them from getting too close, but at least now she could see Him more clearly. Now, if He had the strength to look down, He would know they were there.

The high priest strode their way then, his face smug and dark. His gaze raked over them but just as quickly dismissed them.

He didn't need to punish Magdalene now for her sins—he had done something far worse, and he knew it. He had punished *Jesus* for her sins.

He scowled at something, pointing to the top of the cross. "What is *that*?"

Magdalene hadn't looked beyond her Lord's face, but now she did, her eyes picking out the same message in three languages: *King of the Jews.*

The Sadducee turned to face another man, dressed in Roman fashion. "What were you thinking? You ought to have written, 'This man *said,* I am King of the Jews.'"

The governor, that was who it was. Pontius Pilate. His jaw ticked, and for a moment she thought he would lash out at the priest. But he merely said, "I have written what I have written." Then he pivoted away, leaving the hillside altogether. Justice prescribed, justice delivered, duty done.

As if there was anything just about this.

The priest turned back to the crosses. "Where is Your power and authority now, Rabbi? You who said You could rebuild the Temple in three days? Hmm? Where is Your supposed resurrective power? You raised the dead, You claim—but who faces death now?"

Magdalene wanted to speak, to shout, to proclaim the truth this man so wanted to deny. Jesus *had* raised the dead! She had seen it with her own eyes just months ago in Bethany. She had seen a man four days in his tomb come walking out when the Lord commanded him to arise. She had seen paralytics walk. The blind receive their sight. She had eaten bread multiplied by His prayer.

She had felt her own soul set free and healed.

She didn't dare speak up, not when it could put Imma Mary in danger to do so, but that only made the anger burn hotter inside her.

"Save Yourself, King of the Jews!" someone shouted from behind her in a voice of mockery.

Another sob choked Magdalene. *Save Yourself, King of Heaven!* Her scream may have been silent, but He seemed to hear it, as He always seemed to do. He hung His head, blinked blood and sweat from His eyes, and caught her gaze.

How could love be in His eyes, even now? When agony stretched every feature? When His disciples had fled in fear, when His own people had turned Him over to Rome for death? When even the criminals flanking Him jeered and mocked?

Jesus's eyes slid shut. He opened His mouth, but speaking was no simple matter now. He struggled to draw in a breath, had to lift Himself up to do so, which meant putting weight on His pierced feet to relieve His lungs.

This was the moment. Pushing down her sob, Magdalene gripped Imma Mary's hand and stood up straighter. This was the moment when He would call down the angel armies. The sky, too dark for midday, would flash with terrible light. The very angels that Imma said had appeared above the hills to herald His birth, singing in joy, would appear now with vengeful swords at the ready. He would cry out, and the earth would split, open, devour every faithless person as it had the followers of Korah in the wilderness.

They would all see then. They would all see who He was.

He dragged in a breath, turned His face to heaven, and said, "Father, forgive them. They know not what they do."

"What?" Had she misheard? Was that really what He chose to say with the meager breath He could wrestle from His lungs?

She let go of His mother and sank to her knees, humbled once more. Even now, He taught her. Even now, He met anger with love.

Even now, she had so much to learn.

⁂

THREE YEARS EARLIER

"Are you certain?"

Magdalene had asked that same question of Barnabas several times already that morning. Was he certain that he wanted to stay behind and manage the villa? Was he certain that they could sell the assets he had indicated without harming those who depended on them? Was he certain that she should send a note to her siblings?

She wasn't the one asking the question now though. Khuza stood in her main room, his gaze on his wife, concern and affection weighing down his thick brows.

Theirs had not been a match made for love—they had been betrothed since Joanna was a child, a way of uniting two of the area's leading families. He was twelve years her senior, had already been well established as steward of Herod's household by the time they wed four years ago. It had not taken long, though, for obedience and respect to grow into something far deeper between them. They worked well together, complemented each other, cared for each other as husband and wife should. They grieved together each of three children that had died before they took their first breath.

Separation of even a few weeks would be difficult for them both. But Joanna stood before her husband, their hands entwined, and looked up at him with humble resolution. "I am certain, beloved. I must know more of what He teaches. It will change everything, I know it will. Something in my soul cries out to hear more."

Khuza's larynx bobbed with the force of his swallow. "His teachings align with those of John?"

"They are two branches of the same vine."

Khuza nodded. "You know how I've been pondering the Baptizer's words since I visited him in prison. Would that I had met him when he was free, so that I could have been baptized."

Magdalene, standing at the edge of the room so she didn't intrude, frowned. Khuza had visited John? She hadn't realized.

Of course she hadn't realized—she had been too caught up in the drama of her own wretched life, in trying to win the favor of Alexander, convinced he would set everything to rights. How could she have been so selfish, so oblivious to her friends? For if Khuza visited John, Joanna had known it, they had discussed it. Had she tried to talk about it more with Magdalene?

Joanna smiled at her husband. "From what I've heard, Jesus's disciples are baptizing as well. I will learn all I can in the next few weeks and bring it back to you."

Khuza lifted their joined hands and kissed her knuckles. "I will await your return eagerly." His gaze flicked past her, to Magdalene. "You will take care of her?"

Never in her life had she been directly responsible for the well-being of another, but she nodded, accepting it now with all the sobriety it deserved. "Barnabas has already inquired for us—there is a group of women that travel everywhere with the Rabbi, including His own mother. We will be in good company and well protected."

"Good. Well, then. If you're certain this is what you want to do, beloved, go with my blessing and return with newfound wisdom to share with me."

Somehow the grin Joanna gave him seemed so intimate that Magdalene felt it necessary to slip from the room to provide them with a moment's privacy.

The servants were just returning from the palace, all of her belongings in the trunks they carried, and a trunk full of

Joanna's as well. Neither of them had wanted to return to the palace yesterday, though her friend would have to eventually. Even the thought of stepping foot back in those hallways sent a shiver of dread racing down Magdalene's spine.

She was done with that life. Done with the sin and the temptation and the ambition. Done with the relationships that had never been about people at all, just position. Done with chasing after the wind.

Today marked a new day, with a body and mind healed of her afflictions and, most miraculous of all, a soul washed clean of her sin.

"Who is this man to forgive sins?"

The question had been racing through her mind all through the night, all through the morning thus far. A prophet? Could prophets forgive sins? *"No one but God can do that,"* one of the Pharisees had claimed yesterday.

They should know. The Pharisees studied the sacred Scriptures more than anyone. They knew all the laws, all the statutes, all the prophecies, all the songs. If they said no prophet had such authority, only God Himself, then it was so.

"Where would you like these, mistress? In your bedchamber?"

Magdalene nodded and motioned down the corridor. "Yes, thank you." She wouldn't take much of it with her when she followed after Jesus, of course. According to Barnabas, His retinue traveled on foot, with no wagons or donkeys for their provisions, relying on the people they met along the way to provide for their sustenance. She would take nothing but what she wanted to carry herself. A change of clothes, a few basic necessities for her personal care, and money. Barnabas was visiting the banker even now to withdraw the silver he kept for her.

She held the door open for the line of servants herself, smiling at each one and whispering her thanks to each for his assistance. Many she had known since she was a child, but a few she scarcely recognized, as they had joined the household after she had all but abandoned it to live at court.

Today she saw them all differently. Today she knew that Jesus would go out of His way to heal any one of them. Rich or poor, He made no distinction. He healed the rabble on the streets as surely as He had Magdalene. When she left Simon's home last night, she'd seen a beggar, lame for a decade, dancing— *dancing!*—and singing the praise of Jesus.

Only God could forgive sins.

That Pharisee, then, would say her sins hadn't in fact been forgiven—that if she wanted any hope of such a thing, she would have to journey to Jerusalem and make the appropriate sacrifice at the Temple on the appropriate day and pray that the Lord would be merciful.

Yet even if she did that, those Pharisees wouldn't forgive her. Once one was stained in their eyes, there could be no true redemption. She would be despised forever by them because she had chosen the ways of the Gentiles.

The Pharisees knew all there was to know about Scripture, yes. But they didn't know *this.* They didn't know how it felt to look out at the world and know that not only was she healed, she was *clean.* She was new. She'd been reborn. That regeneration had started when Jesus cast the demons from her, but it had been completed when He looked into her eyes last night and said those precious words: *"Your sins are forgiven."*

Only God could forgive sins, yes—but He had done it through Jesus. She knew He had. She felt the weightlessness of it, the relief, the light. True light, which not only cast out the darkness, it shone so that those shadows could never find harbor within her again.

Once all the servants had returned to their normal duties, she slipped into her bedchamber and went straight for the small sack she'd already decided would be her only bag. She would take nothing that wouldn't fit inside it. Already she'd changed out of her stola, putting the more traditional Jewish garment on over her tunic and a scarf over her hair.

Mary again. The girl she'd been when Abba lived. The girl she'd put away after she stumbled into the pool of his blood.

She brought the images up deliberately this time, testing herself. The horror still lingered. The pain was still a dull pulse in her heart. But neither consumed her. Neither threatened to send her in search of darkness to obliterate it.

"Thank You, Lord God." She drew in a breath that tasted of a thousand new tomorrows and let it back out with a smile. Had her abba been here now, he would have loved to hear Jesus. He would have been the first in Magdala to invite Him to dine, and he wouldn't have treated Him as Simon had. Abba had always been the first to tend to the needs of the poor, and any teacher who did the same would have only risen in his estimation.

It took only a few minutes to fold up her change of clothes and tuck it and the other items into her bag. She didn't bother with any longing looks at the rest of her things. They were only that—*things*. She was in pursuit of something far greater now.

By the time she made her way back to the main part of the house, Joanna had transferred her necessary items to a small bag too, and Barnabas was standing at the door with several leather money pouches.

He held out one on a long string. "Wear this one around your neck, mistress."

She took it and slid it over her head, tucking it under her loose, concealing clothing.

"This one is for you to keep in your bag." He handed over the second, which she tucked into the bottom of her sack. "I have already entrusted one to Joanna. This final one you should give directly to the disciple who manages their money box. It is best if it is not all kept in one place, in case you encounter bandits."

She nodded, but the thought of being accosted by criminals on the road held no terror for her. Demons, after all, had run screaming from the presence of Jesus. How could men stand before Him if He commanded them to depart? She would be safe as long as she was in His company, of that she hadn't the slightest doubt. He was clearly on a mission from God Himself, and nothing would stand in the way of that.

"Thank you, Barnabas. For everything." She leaned down and picked up one of the two waterskins awaiting them. Joanna slid the strap of the other over her shoulder.

Her steward offered her a fatherly smile. "It is my pleasure to serve you, and it will be my delight to hear your stories of the Lord Jesus whenever you return."

"I will commit all I learn to memory so that I can share it with you. I'll even write to you whenever I can." She knew her own smile was more excitement than sorrow at the parting. "Are you ready, Joanna?"

"I am." Her friend gave Khuza one last embrace and then stepped to Magdalene's side. "We had better go so we don't miss them."

They hurried out into the sunshine and onto the road they'd traveled together so often, between the villa and the town. Though Herod's palace loomed on the next hill over, Magdalene felt no need to look in that direction today. She didn't care who might be coming or going, what they were wearing, or what gossip they might carry and call news. None of it mattered. She'd been a fool ever to think it did.

Instead her eyes scanned the road in search of the party that would soon become their companions. When she'd asked their plans last night, Jesus said His group would be leaving Magdala midmorning and traveling north, where they would meet up at the next town with the disciples He'd apparently sent out several weeks ago to work on His behalf.

Her blood thrummed in her veins as they walked, growing louder as she spotted a group leaving the town on the northbound road. "There. That must be them!"

CHAPTER NINE

For a moment Magdalene feared they wouldn't actually catch up with the group, but they seemed to be in no great hurry now. They'd paused beside a stream, no doubt to fill waterskins. As they drew closer, Magdalene noted with relief the figures she recognized—Jesus, James, John, and Peter. Nearly as interesting to her, though, were the ones bending now beside the water, their figures feminine. These would be her companions, she knew.

For the first time since she made the decision last night to follow Jesus as He left the area, a wisp of anxiety curled around her. She hadn't had the best of luck making friends with other women. Joanna and Salome were the only two she could really boast. All the other women of Herodias's throng had considered her a rival, and the Jewish girls she'd grown up with had always been more acquaintances than friends. Even with her own sister, she'd argued more than gotten along.

What if these women didn't like her? Would she really be able to follow the Rabbi if His current followers declared her an unfit companion?

The wisp of worry didn't linger though, certainly didn't strangle her as her anxieties had been doing for the last three years. It was there, but just a whiff she caught when she moved her head, barely present.

When He spotted them, Jesus lifted a hand in greeting, His smile rivaling the sun for brightness and warmth. "Mary and Joanna! How good it is to see you."

The other women turned quickly enough that Magdalene wondered what the men had said about them last night. Whatever they had heard, their smiles were just as bright and welcoming as Jesus's.

She thought she saw a resemblance between the Rabbi and the woman in the middle of the feminine trio—she was lovely, probably in her midforties, with the kindest eyes Magdalene had ever seen. The woman to her right looked to be a bit older, the hair escaping her headscarf a silver-white. The third was younger, probably only a year or two older than Magdalene.

The middle woman came forward, her hands extended in welcome. "Good morning, my friends. How lovely to meet you at last. My Son told us to expect you."

The words sent that wisp of worry blowing away in the wind and brought a new smile to Magdalene's lips. She took the woman's hands in her own. "You must be the Rabbi's mother."

"Mary," she confirmed with a smile that grew into a grin as she nodded toward her older companion. "Though my friend is also Mary—mother of James and John, two of my Son's followers. And you are as well, so this could get very confusing."

Laughter tickled her throat. "How fortunate then that I answer most often to Magdalene. You're welcome to call me that."

"I shall. And you may simply call me Imma, as most of the boys do, since Jesus does. Or Imma Mary. That leaves the simple 'Mary' for our elder."

The other Mary narrowed her eyes, though she was clearly more amused than offended at being called out as the eldest among them. "I may be the eldest of the group, but I can still keep pace with young Susanna here, can't I?"

Susanna directed her grin to Magdalene and Joanna. "The Rabbi healed my twisted foot. I never dreamed of keeping up with able-bodied people, much less setting the pace."

Another woman healed by the Teacher, and two mothers. Magdalene couldn't have pieced together a better collection had she tried. "Joanna and I would like to travel with you all for a while, if we may."

"Of course you may!" Imma Mary beamed and linked their arms together. "We never deny any who wish to follow my Son—just know that it isn't an easy life. We live as nomads, especially when our journeying takes us out of Galilee and away from our family homes."

Joanna said, "I personally will only be able to follow within the region. When you leave Galilee, I will have to remain behind and return to my husband."

Imma smiled. "You will be welcome whenever you can join us, and when you must depart, it will be with our well-wishes for you and your husband."

By rights, Magdalene should have been uneasy at the warning of a difficult life. What did she know of living like a nomad? Nothing. She knew how to plan a meal for a household and had assisted with the preparation of it plenty of times—Abba insisted his daughters know all the skills that would ensure they'd make fine wives—but that assumed an oven and satchels full of herbs and spices, servants to bring her flour, milk, butter, oil, and fresh meat. Out here? She didn't know the first thing about living on the road.

She would learn though. She would learn anything she must.

"Is everyone ready?" From His place a few paces away, Jesus surveyed their small group as He slung His now-filled waterskin over His shoulder. "We will reunite with Andrew and Bartholomew by dark if we set a good pace."

Imma Mary turned back for her own water, though Jesus lifted it from her hands before she could slip it over her head. She gave Him one of those looks Magdalene had seen other mothers give their sons—looks that said they could have done a task themselves but appreciated the help simply because their child thought to extend it. A proud, amused, half-chiding look that spoke of the deepest affection.

The youngest-looking disciple, John, moved forward with his hand outstretched. "I can take it, my Lord." He took the other Mary's waterskin from her too and slung it over his back, and seeing them side by side revealed that he had her eyes and smile. Was she *his* mother, perhaps?

Jesus waved him away. "If ever I'm unable, John, you can help My mother. For now, it's My joy and privilege."

With the Teacher in the lead, their group set off again, this time at a good pace. Magdalene knew she'd be exhausted physically by the end of the day, likely with a few blisters on her pampered feet. Even so, she was looking forward to every step. "Does He teach as we walk?" she asked of His mother in an undertone.

Imma Mary chuckled. "You'll find my Son teaches in all He does—occasionally with words, always with actions. It's been this way since He was a babe—I think I've learned more from Him than I've taught Him. Though since His cousin John baptized Him a few months ago..." She broke off, shaking her head, a new light in her eyes. "He has stepped fully now into the role I have waited these thirty years to see Him take up."

"His *cousin?*" Joanna exchanged a horrified look with Magdalene. "John the Baptizer was His cousin?"

Did they know of his beheading? If not, that past-tense *was* of Joanna's would upset them terribly. But Imma showed no surprise, only sorrow as she nodded. "He was the son of my cousin Elizabeth. I was there for his birth, just six months before Jesus's. I will never forget the joy in his mother's eyes as she held that long-awaited child. Both she and her husband knew that he would be remarkable. It was promised to them by an angel."

Magdalene nearly stumbled over her own feet. "An angel?"

"Zechariah was visited while he was ministering to the Lord. The angel told him his wife would have a son, even though they were both old and well past childbearing years. The angel said this son would be a great prophet. He was even instructed to name him John."

"I can scarcely imagine. And yet..." Joanna gave Magdalene's elbow a squeeze. "I know they exist, just as demons do. It is reassuring to hear that they continue to proclaim the messages of God. I have never met anyone before who has seen one."

"You have now." Imma kept her gaze on her Son's back, though her face said she was seeing something different, perhaps long past. "I have entertained a heavenly visitor myself. He announced my Son's birth as well."

Perhaps a week ago Magdalene would have been dubious of such a claim. After all, they no longer lived in the age of the prophets. Angels didn't simply swoop down anymore to tell women they would be delivering sons.

But this Son? A Son who could cast out demons and forgive sins? Of course angels proclaimed Him. They probably marched alongside Him even now, ministering to Him. Perhaps if she had the eyes to see, she'd catch a glimpse of them.

She looked around, waiting for a shimmer to give one away, but all she saw were the birds flitting overhead, the grass bending in the wind, and a group of travelers approaching them on the road, from the direction of Herod's palace.

Her stomach tightened. She'd hoped she would be able to escape the area without running into anyone from the court. Perhaps it would be no one she knew. Or at the very least, no one who would recognize her now in her modest clothes.

"Joanna? *Magdalene?*"

She jumped a bit at the voice, far closer than the group she'd just noticed. Alexander stood but a stone's throw away, incredulity on his face. He'd come to a halt in the middle of the road, a well-loaded donkey behind him, its reins in the hand of a servant. He was gaping at them as though he thought himself hallucinating.

Magdalene mustered up a smile. "Good day, Alexander. Are you leaving the palace?"

"The birthday feast is over, so yes—I'm departing to take possession of the villa ten miles hence that my father purchased."

She'd heard all about that villa, and he'd promised her a trip to it someday. It had seemed a bright, shining thing at the time, a promise of a shared future. Now she could nod without the slightest curiosity about it. "I hope you find it in good condition."

"I anticipate no problems that a firm managerial hand will not put to rights." He glanced at the others in the group—the three women, dismissed in a moment, the three men, who actually made his lip curl up in disgust. "Who are these men? Are they servants of yours?"

A laugh slipped out before she could stifle it. "No. No, quite the contrary. I am here to learn from the Teacher." She inclined her head toward Jesus, who had come to a halt along the edge of the road to let the donkey pass and watched with that frank, knowing way she was coming to discover was typical of Him.

Alexander sent a quick, measuring glance over Him, from tip to toe. How, then, did he manage to dismiss Him with another sneer? How could he not see the intelligence and wisdom and authority in His eyes? "A teacher? I see only a…a fisherman, perhaps."

Jesus seemed to be fighting a grin. "Carpenter, actually. Though My friends here are fishermen, so you aren't entirely wrong. About *that*, anyway." He tilted His head to the side. "There are plenty other things about which you're mistaken, though, My friend. Join us for a mile or two, if you like. We can talk about the questions you have."

Alexander scoffed a laugh. "As if You know a thing about me."

"I know that you fear you will be a disappointment to your father. I know that you question whether obeying all the Law will truly be enough to win you salvation. I know you despair of ever finding a wife who won't betray you as your mother did your father."

Alexander's eyes flashed with cold, hard fury—fury he sent toward Magdalene. "Is this how you repay me for my attention? You gossip about me with every man who comes along?"

Magdalene's stomach tightened again but not in the way she knew so well. Not with anger, nor with worry. Rather, with sorrow. "How could I have? You never told me any of that." If those were his worries, though, then Magdalene had been the worst possible thing for him. What had she done but prove his fears valid? Yet there *was* hope of salvation—he would discover that as she did, if he but walked a mile with Jesus. "Walk with us, Alexander. Please. Listen to what Jesus has to say—it will leave you changed."

Alexander shook his head, his face grim. "I'll walk nowhere with the likes of you."

"Then I'll stay behind! Only go. Please. I offer it as my apology to you." She could always catch up with this group farther along the road, if her presence was deterring Alexander. She didn't want to be the thing between him and a miracle of his own. He needed the peace, forgiveness, and healing that Jesus offered too.

He narrowed his eyes, looking from her headscarf to her clothing and then back to her face. "What has gotten into you?"

"Peace. Joy. Hope—all in the place of the evil that left me when I fell at the Teacher's feet and begged for healing. He delivered me from my torment. He forgave me for my many sins."

The fury only compounded. "*He* forgave you for your sins? It was not Him you sinned against! You do not *deserve* to be forgiven!"

"Who does?" Jesus spoke softly, but there was something more than friendliness in His eyes now. "Forgiveness is a gift of which no one is truly worthy—but it is a gift, given because the Father loves us."

"You don't know. You don't know the kind of woman You've invited in Your company."

"I know exactly the kind of woman she is—a sinner washed clean by the grace of God, who knows to whom she owes her life."

Her heart glowed even as it ached for Alexander. "I am sorry I hurt you, Alexander. I am sorry I was not who you thought me."

"But you are now, is that what you'll claim? That you've changed? You deserve another chance?" He snatched the donkey's reins from the servant and gave them a hard yank that, predictably, made the donkey dig in its heels and bray an objection to the treatment.

"I have changed. But I would not ask for a second chance." She could not possibly think of things like marriage now—she had too much to learn, too many questions, too much yearning for things no mere man could offer.

Alexander jerked the reins again. When the donkey stubbornly pulled against him, he threw the leather back to the servant and spun on Jesus. "Tell her to leave. Banish her from Your company forever, and then I'll travel with You for a while and hear what You have to say."

Jesus's eyes burned. "Careful, friend. You will be judged by the Father in heaven with the same judgment you offer others on earth. If you crave His mercy, you must extend your own."

Alexander crossed his arms over his chest. "Those are my terms. If You want to speak with me, then You must tell her to leave."

"Alexander, Alexander." Jesus shook His head, sorrow overtaking His voice. "No one who seeks My company will ever be turned away. No one who would repent and embrace salvation will ever be denied it. And no one who would wish the torments of hell on another soul will ever themselves see heaven."

Alexander backed away another step. "You act as though You know a thing about it—but who are You to proclaim such things?"

A bit of Jesus's amusement returned. "That seems to be the question of the week—perhaps the question of the ages. A question each much answer for himself."

The tallest of the disciples stepped forward with a grin. He looked older than Jesus by about a decade and did indeed wear the simple clothing of a fisherman. "I can tell him who You are—my Lord and Master, the one who has the answers."

Jesus chuckled. "Which will mean very little to him, Peter, even if you proclaim it from the rooftops."

Alexander pivoted back toward the south, toward Magdala, away from them. "I have no more time to waste on such folly. I thank You to stay out of the way of my retinue when they pass You by."

"You speak rightly, that you have no time for folly. If only you knew what folly truly was." With a sigh, Jesus moved farther off the road, into the grass. "Pass by, friend, if that is what you wish. We'll not stand in your way."

Magdalene moved aside along with the other women. One part of her wanted to look down, the shame of how she'd treated Alexander—and even of what she'd expected of him, which he never could have given—heavy and guilty. But the greater part followed him with her gaze as he strode by, praying he would change his mind.

He needed to know what Jesus taught. Everyone needed to know.

Imma Mary reached out and clasped Magdalene's hand in her own. "Pray for him, my daughter. Pray every day that he will see the light and chase after it. Pray he does not give in to the shadows chasing after *him*."

Magdalene could only nod.

CHAPTER TEN

The fires crackled merrily in the camp—one in the center where the men were gathered, one farther off that the women were using for cooking, several around the edges where different families and groups gathered. One of the disciples strummed a familiar tune on his lyre, and all around the camp people lifted their voices in the words of praise to God.

Let them praise his name in the dance: let them sing praises unto him with the timbrel and harp.

For the Lord taketh pleasure in his people: he will beautify the meek with salvation.

Let the saints be joyful in glory: let them sing aloud upon their beds.

Magdalene hummed along with the music but left the lyrics to the others tonight lest trying to remember them steal her focus. Last week she'd given herself a nice slice to her thumb thanks to her inattentiveness to her vegetable chopping. She'd learned her lesson: when she was helping cook, others could sing.

She swept the root vegetable she'd just finished dicing into the cookpot and dared a glance up. Over the twelve days she'd been with the group, it had swollen from the six she'd seen on the road outside Magdala to more than eighty. Men and women, young and old, some from Galilee, others from far afield.

All here to learn from Jesus—not just to listen to the sermons He delivered to the crowds during the day but to watch Him, as His mother had said. To see how He lived the lessons He taught. To gather together each spare word that dripped from His lips and store them like the treasure they were.

The Rabbi sat now by the central fire, saying something she couldn't hear over the song, gesturing widely as He spoke. Whatever it was earned a laugh from the knot of disciples closest to Him—closest in proximity and in trust. The Twelve, the rest of them called them. The ones He had called by name to leave their professions and walk with Him. The ones that He took aside to explain more than the rest of them ever heard. The ones so blessed as to stay at His side even when He dismissed the crowds.

Soft laughter drew her attention back to the stack of vegetables still waiting to be turned into dinner. Imma Mary had appeared at her side and was pulling the knife from Magdalene's fingers. "I'll finish these."

Her cheeks flushed. It was her turn to help—they all took their turns. "No, you needn't. I'll do it. I'm happy to."

"I know you are." Imma smiled. "But I have another task for you—little Nahara fell on her way back from the river and could use some of that balm you used on her sister the other day."

"Oh, of course." Magdalene relinquished the knife without any more fuss and pushed to her feet. She couldn't even argue that she'd finish this task first, nor that she would come back to it. Both were of equal urgency, after all. Though even so, she hated to add more work to Imma Mary's list of chores. She was always busier than any of them, acting as hostess to the gathering, no matter how many new faces showed up for a meal.

Magdalene scarcely remembered her own mother. Sarah had been too young to really step into the role when their imma died, and she and Magdalene had been butting heads most of their lives, having dispositions that constantly clashed. Having a mother always at hand now had proven nearly as much a blessing as learning from the Rabbi Himself. Jesus certainly taught her how to be a person after the heart of God—but Imma Mary showed her how to be a good woman too. The sort King Solomon had praised in Proverbs. The kind who knew how to minister physically to the people who came to Jesus for the needs of their spirits.

Magdalene could only pray to be that sort of woman someday.

For now, little Nahara. She went first to her bag and fished out the small jar of balm she'd brought with her. It was her own imma's recipe, one that their family swore by and which she'd never for a moment considered leaving home without. It had always traveled with her to the palace, and it would travel with her now too. When this jar ran empty, she would purchase the honey, oil, and herbs to make a new batch.

She found the girl with her family at the edge of the camp, curled up in her mother's lap with a scraped and bloodied leg dangling down. She was no longer crying, but her cheeks bore the tracks of tears and her eyes the puffiness.

Sharelle, Nahara's mother, looked up at Magdalene with a grateful sigh. "Did Imma Mary send you?"

Magdalene nodded and brandished her jar. "I come bearing a gift. May I?" She crouched down in front of the girl and looked at her leg in the last light of the setting sun. Sharelle must have already cleaned it—no dirt or grass or stones clung to the broken skin.

Nahara sniffled and hooked a finger in her mouth. "Hurts, Magda."

"I know, sweet girl. I took my share of tumbles as a child too." She held up the jar for her to see. "Do you remember this? I used it on your sister the other day when she burned her hand?"

Nahara nodded. "Smells good. She said it didn't sting."

"That's right. It may sting just a bit as I'm putting it on—not the balm itself, but just because I have to touch where it hurts. Will you still try to sit still for me while I apply it? Then your imma will wrap a bandage around your leg to protect it, and it'll start feeling better in a few days."

Nahara's lip wobbled. "I don't want you to touch it. Can't you make it better without touching it?"

Poor, sweet child. Magdalene brushed back a lock of the girl's hair that was stuck to her face by the salt from her tears. "Would that it worked that way, dear one. I'm afraid our hurts never get better without touching them. We must wash them clean, as your mother has already done. We must put medicine on them. We must wrap them up to keep more dirt from getting in. That's how they stop hurting."

A lesson for more pains than physical ones. A lesson she had stridently refused to learn when it came to the wounds on her heart and soul after her father's murder.

Nahara turned her face into her mother's chest, and Sharelle nodded her permission to apply the balm. Magdalene dabbed her finger into it. "Tell me about your visit to the river. Did you see any animals while you were down there? Any fish in the waters?"

Nahara was always the first to exclaim when a bird swooped overhead or they startled a deer from its hiding place, and the question served to distract her just enough. She wasn't as chatty as usual about the creatures she'd spotted, but she at least listed them as Magdalene gently smoothed the balm over her leg. It only took a minute, and then she withdrew her hand with a smile.

"There. You were very brave, Nahara. We'll apply more tomorrow evening, all right?"

The girl nodded, Sharelle mouthed her thanks, and Magdalene slipped away, back to the space she'd claimed for her blanket and bag, between Joanna's and Susanna's spots. She returned the balm to her bag and then moved back to the women and the cookpots to find whatever task needed her attention.

At least that's what she meant to do. Except that the singers had gone silent, and with only the soft strumming of the lyre in the background, Jesus's voice reached her. Tugged her. Pulled her over until she'd crept to the edge of the circle of disciples around the fire.

John's disciples were counted among their number now too. They had joined up with them the same day that Magdalene and Joanna had, after burying their master's body. Jesus had withdrawn from them for a while after that, walking on His own, His face lifted to heaven.

Was He praying? Mourning? Angry with Herod and Herodias?

She didn't know—only that when He returned, more of His own disciples had found Him, as He'd predicted, and He declared that they would be journeying by boat across the Sea of Galilee for a few weeks of quiet.

Magdalene had been dismayed, certain that Joanna would leave after only a day on the road together—but she ought to have known better. Her friend wasn't about to depart before she even heard another of His sermons. So they had shared a boat with the other women and crossed the sea, and ever since then she'd been laughing at the Teacher's goal of weeks of "quiet."

In every town they passed, people not only ran out to meet them and hear Him speak, but some stayed with them, unwilling to leave again so soon. Tomorrow they would be passing by a city, not just a town—how many would spill out of the walls and gates to see Him? To hear Him?

Hundreds, at the least. Thousands, perhaps.

"Master." Another of the Twelve approached—Judas, with a look of worry on his face. "If I may have a moment?"

Jesus turned His full attention to the man, though He didn't rise. "Of course, My friend. What is it that has your brow creased with worry?"

Judas sighed. "Master, the group continues to grow, and no one comes with provisions of their own. You should dismiss them all back to their homes in the morning. We haven't enough to feed them."

For a moment, Jesus held His disciple's gaze. Then He looked out over the throng of people gathered together against the encroaching night. "They are desperate people, My friend. Desperate for hope. Desperate for healing. Desperate to know more of My Father. How can I turn them away?"

"Not forever, my Lord! Not when You are speaking to them, but…they still need to eat, don't they?"

"As do the birds of the air. The deer of the fields. The fish of the sea. Do you see them carrying money bags or stew pots?" The Rabbi's eyes twinkled. "My Father cares for them—He will care for us. For all of these."

Judas sighed again, and it sounded more like defeat than that he was convinced. He glanced over and apparently just noticed Magdalene nearby, given the sour expression that flashed across his face.

Judas had not been happy to find her and Joanna among their number when he returned from being sent out. He was from Galilee—he'd known their names, if not their faces. He'd known they'd come from Herod's palace. He'd apparently heard plenty of other rumors about "the lady of Magdala" too, given the way he'd reacted.

He'd looked every bit as pained as little Nahara when he had to accept her donation for the money box that he kept. As if her silver was as stained as her past. He'd refused much of it, in fact, taking only a few coins and making her keep the rest "for her journey home."

She hadn't told him she had plenty more, though she'd confided it to Jesus and His mother.

Not that it did them much good out here in the wilderness, where there were no towns to buy provisions. Someone always went into the towns they passed to get supplies, but they hadn't passed anything today. They would skirt the city tomorrow, though.

Judas stalked toward her. He'd have to ask for the rest of the money, and for a moment she felt a jolt of satisfaction at the realization that he'd be humbled.

No—that wasn't right. She swallowed it down like the bile it was and tried to find a smile for him instead. *Gracious*, she told herself. *Be gracious. Be generous. Remember that he has every right to think as he does about you.*

"What are you doing here, woman?" he snapped at her. "Shouldn't you be helping the others with the meal?"

What? Magdalene could only gape at him.

"Useless." With that, he strode off.

"Judas!" Jesus's shout brought sudden silence to the camp, silence that made Magdalene's throat tighten even as her heart pulsed painfully in her chest. He'd stood, the dual lights of the fire and the dying sun casting a golden glow around Him, illumining the suddenly hard lines of His face.

Judas halted. Paused. Turned. "Yes, Master?"

Jesus said nothing for a long moment. "Do you know what is required in this life?"

A lesson—the sort He gave so freely, so frequently. Judas inclined his head, his shoulders relaxing. "What is required?"

"Mary knows."

Judas's head snapped up again, his nostrils flaring. "I beg your pardon?"

Their Teacher held out a hand toward her. "Mary knows. Ask her. Ask her where she should be."

Silence. Mary tried to swallow, tried to calm the burning at the back of her neck, but it was no use. Dozens of sets of eyes were on her, and no headscarf in the world was large enough to shield her from them.

But Jesus's eyes were on her too, and she never wanted to shield herself from Him. They smiled at her now, even though His lips didn't. "Tell them, Mary. Where is it you want to be?"

Only one answer came to mind, and it sprang to her lips in a joyful whisper. "At Your feet, Master."

He nodded. "And so you shall remain. No one will forbid you that."

Grateful tears stung her eyes, and she lowered her head. He had taken her part—against one of the Twelve. But it wasn't for anything she'd done, not for anything she was. He'd taken her part because everyone needed to know that He'd never turn them away. Everyone needed to know that there was no better place for them to be.

Even so, that did nothing to diminish the gratitude that rose up in her again. The Teacher who served the masses welcomed her too. The Rabbi who gathered crowds also took the time to affirm one woman who was out of her depth.

And in so doing, He put a finger on the thing that had been niggling her as her feet blistered and the blisters turned to calluses, as she followed along on paths she'd never trod and wondered when Imma Mary or Mary or Susanna or the others would grow weary of her.

She'd been wondering, all these twelve days, where she really belonged—in the world, in His retinue, in her own family.

Now she had her answer. And it was one she would never again doubt.

She had been right to guess that thousands would turn out to hear Him. The next day Magdalene sat with the other woman on a hillside and marveled at the sea of people strewn about the valley. There were thousands. Thousands upon thousands. Perhaps tens of thousands, how was she to know? How did one count a multitude this large? They filled the valley, covered the hills like a blanket of wildflowers in every color.

Jesus had been teaching for hours already, His voice carrying out over the people with the clarity of a bell, reaching far and wide. He'd finally paused, healing a few of the supplicants who had climbed up to reach for Him.

Four of His disciples strode toward the group Magdalene had been sitting with, which included three more of the Twelve. They looked…perplexed. Perhaps even worried. The remaining five soon drifted their way too.

"It's getting late," Andrew said, measuring the time with a hand lifted against the horizon. "The people are hungry."

"I told the Lord to dismiss the crowd, but He wouldn't." Peter rubbed a hand over his face and down his beard. "He told *us* to feed them."

Judas snorted. "Feed them what? Isn't this what I said last night? We haven't provisions enough, and there isn't anywhere nearby where we could possibly get food enough for this crowd. Even if we spent all the money dear *Magdalene's* estates bring in in a year, it wouldn't be enough." He shot her a scowl.

Her cheeks burned. It seemed that Jesus's words last night hadn't made Judas soften toward her—quite the opposite. He'd cast her nothing but dark looks all day.

She lifted her brows. "If my money would have been useful, the Teacher would have instructed me to give it and you to spend it. He didn't, because He knew well it would be useless."

"That is exactly what I—"

"Which means He has a different answer. An answer that will bring glory to God." Her gaze darted to Imma Mary beside her. "Right?"

The matriarch grinned. "Exactly right. What did my Son say to do?"

Peter waved a hand. "He said to bring Him what we have."

"Then I will tell you what I told the servants at the wedding feast in Cana—do what He told you to do." She lifted her brows and made an amused shooing motion with her hands.

Magdalene had already heard the story of the miracle Jesus had performed several months ago, turning the giant urns of water on hand for the wedding guests' washing into the finest wine any of them had ever tasted. He'd saved a family from disgrace that day, and honored the petition of His precious mother.

It was just like Him. Magdalene had had no trouble at all believing He would do such a thing, nor that He could. Not having felt for herself the power He could harness at will.

"Who is this man?"

She heard the question wherever they went, after every miracle, every healing, every teaching. She heard it in her own heart every day too. She turned over each possible answer. Prophet? King?

God?

Blasphemy, that last thought. But she didn't know how else to reconcile the truth her soul knew with the truths the Scriptures taught. Only God could do the things Jesus did. But He did them. Which meant…?

She turned to Imma Mary, trying again to find the courage to ask the questions she'd been wrestling with for nearly two weeks. "Imma?"

Now was surely not the time to ask. Not with thousands of people around and the Twelve scraping together the few loaves and fish that one of their younger brothers had brought with him that morning. Not, with Judas still glaring at her.

But Imma looked over at her, expectant, smiling. "Yes, daughter?"

Magdalene glanced at Joanna for support. They'd whispered the questions to each other as they walked, and as they tried to find rest at night despite twitching, overused leg muscles and bleeding feet. Joanna lifted her brows, tilted her head, as if to say, *If you think you should, go ahead.*

Magdalene scooted a little closer. "You've told us about your Son as He is now—that first miracle He performed, the others that came after, before we joined you. You've told us that your cousin Elizabeth's husband was told by an angel that John would be born to them, and that he would be a herald of God. You said you too had been visited by an angel. Would you…would you tell us of that? Did the angel visit your husband as well?"

She knew very little of Joseph—only that he'd been a carpenter, that Jesus had loved him, that He and His mother had mourned together when he died six months ago…and that after their mourning was complete, Jesus had closed up the carpentry shop and started this new journey.

That still left thirty years of mystery. Did the answer to who or what He truly was lie somewhere in those years?

Imma's face softened, distant…glowing. "In a dream, yes. Months after his visit to me. To assure my dear Joseph that I hadn't betrayed him, that he needn't divorce me, despite…" She blinked the memories from her eyes and leaned closer. "The miracles did not begin with water turned to wine, my daughters. The miracle began with His very conception. Joseph and I were betrothed but not yet married, and I had never known a man. But the angel came. Called me blessed. And said that I would conceive, not by man but by the Spirit of God, if I but said yes."

Ten thousand voices might have been speaking around her, but Magdalene heard none of them. Ten thousand faces might have been laughing or weeping or sleeping, but she could see only the one of the woman before her, radiating remembered glory.

Ten thousand doubts might have flown at her like fiery darts—but they all hissed out, extinguished, knocked from the air by one simple truth.

Only God could forgive sins. Only God could command demons and be obeyed. Only God could rewrite the very laws of nature. God and this man called Jesus.

His…Son.

His *Son?* God had a Son? Born of a woman—this woman, who had said an impossible *yes*. Magdalene's breath came in ragged. "You…you said yes. Though it could have meant your death. Divorce. Shame."

Imma reached for their hands, hers and Joanna's, and gripped them. "I said yes. Trusting that if the God of the universe wanted His Son to be born of my body, then He would protect it. He would make a way for us. He would be my pillar of fire by night and my cloud by day, guiding my feet, sheltering me. And so He did." She looked over her shoulder, to her Son.

God's Son. Jesus was even then taking the few paltry loaves and fish from Peter's hands and raising them to heaven. He said a blessing over them, His voice carrying out over the valley once again.

Joanna's free hand gripped Magdalene's, linking them into a circle. "What does that mean—that God is His father? That He is not human?"

Imma squeezed their hands. "He is human. I changed His diapers, I nursed Him, I kissed His knees when He fell. He is flesh and bone and has a nature like ours. One that hungers and thirsts and weeps and laughs. And yet…"

"He is more than that too." Magdalene watched as He lifted one of the small loaves from the basket and broke it in half and then picked up another and broke it too. Then another, and another, when there should have been no more. Again. And again. Always pulling out a whole loaf where there should have been only broken pieces. Always turning that one into two. Somehow, in His hands, the bread didn't divide, it multiplied.

Somehow, in His hands, the few small, dried fish did the same.

Somehow, in His hands, the whole face of the world was reshaped.

Fully man…but fully God. Somehow. Some way. By some miracle. God had taken on flesh. *That* flesh, before her now. He had come down from heaven to walk the earth. To feed these hungry people. To heal their broken bodies. To free their enslaved souls.

He'd come for them, because He loved them.

He'd come for *her.*

In a few short minutes, Jesus had filled basket upon basket with food and instructed the Twelve to organize the people and give the bread and fish to them. But to their small group He came Himself, a smile on His face and a twinkle in His eye.

He held out a crusty, fragrant half loaf of bread to them. "Hungry, Imma?"

Imma Mary took the loaf from His hands, breathing a laugh as she did so. "It is fresh."

"Of course it's fresh."

"The loaves Joses had were two days old. Hard. Cold."

He grinned. "You think I would feed My mother cold, hard bread?"

She chuckled, broke a piece off, and handed it to Joanna. "I tasted Your wine, my Son—I know You create only the best."

Create—that's what He was doing. Creating something from nothing, as He must have done alongside the Father in heaven at the start of the world. Her head swam. And yet she knew it was true.

She knew it because He had created new life within her too.

Joanna passed Magdalene the loaf—still a perfect half, despite the pieces they'd torn off. She tore a chunk of her own too, and reached over her shoulder to give it to Susanna. She looked up at Jesus.

Jesus—the Son of God. The Son of Mary, but the *Son of God.*

He smiled. "Are your questions answered, Mary?"

She held the warm loaf in her hands, felt it flex under her fingers like a loaf fresh from the oven, smelled its fragrance rising on the air. "They are, Lord."

"Good. Then eat—you're going to need your strength."

A warning? Perhaps. But if He said she needed strength, then He would grant it to her. She lifted the bread to her lips, took a bite…and wondered if this was what manna had tasted like in the wilderness.

CHAPTER ELEVEN

FRIDAY

No angels seared the skies with their glory and light. But the earth shook under their feet, the midday sun dark as twilight. The whole earth revolted.

Magdalene and her companions had all sunk to the ground at its quaking, clinging to each other to keep from getting tossed down. Thunder roared all around them, and she swore she heard the gleeful keening of demons on the wind. Rejoicing at their victory.

The Lord's every breath grew harder, more labored.

He was going to die. If He didn't do something soon to stop it, they would win. He would die. And then what? How could life possibly go on if He wasn't in it? Would the earth in fact fall to pieces? Would God give up on humanity, punish them for slaying His beloved Son, destroy them all as He swore after the days of Noah that He wouldn't do?

"Did you know?" she whispered to Imma Mary as one moment stretched into the next. "Did you know all He would do?"

Imma shook her head, her gaze never leaving her Son's face. "I knew He was the Son of God. I knew that made Him the most remarkable Person in history. I knew that He would do things no one else ever had. But how could I know what it would look like? God had never taken on flesh before."

Magdalene too kept her gaze on Jesus. "What does it mean? That He is dying? I don't understand. I don't understand how the Son of God can die. He should be immortal. I thought…I suppose I thought He would live forever. As He promised all of us we would."

Impossible, but she had believed it because He said it.

Imma shook her head again. "I don't know, my daughter. I don't know what any of it means. I know only that man in all his schemes cannot undo the will of God. The high priests cannot circumvent His plan. Which means this must be part of it."

This? No. "No. God could not want this. He could not want Jesus to suffer like this. It isn't right!"

On the cross before them, Jesus convulsed. *"Eloi, Eloi, lema sabachthani?"*

"No!" Magdalene cried again. God couldn't have abandoned Him! He was His Son! Fathers didn't just abandon their sons!

Except they did, all the time. Death always came between fathers and their children. But the heavenly Father was supposed to be different. Wasn't that what Jesus had promised? That God would never leave them, never forsake them? That He loved them so much that He sent Jesus here to save them?

Like the bronze serpent that Moses raised up for the Israelites in the wilderness, that was what Jesus had said. Just like their ancestors, salvation was provided, if they but had faith enough to look upon it.

She had been bitten, bitten by the serpent of sin. She had been dying from its venom, little by little. But she had looked upon Jesus and trusted, and He had made her whole again.

Her throat went dry. Moses hadn't just fastened the metal serpent to the staff—he had lifted it up high for all the people to see. She had thought, when Jesus made the analogy, that His own "lifting high" would be metaphorical. That He would be raised up before the people in victory.

Not on a cross, fastened to it like that lifeless snake.

"My God, My God, why have You forsaken Me?"

Did Jesus really feel forsaken by the Father God, even though He always spoke so intimately of Him? *Was* He really forsaken by Him?

She glanced over and saw that tears were streaming down Imma Mary's beautiful face. "My Son," she whispered. "My Son. You are ever beloved."

Jesus's head fell again, rolled a moment from side to side. The blood had stopped oozing from the crown of thorns, and its tracks had dried to dark lines down His face, His neck, His torso. His blinks seemed to take three times as long as they should have, but with great effort He focused His gaze upon Imma Mary.

A lifetime must have passed between them in that moment. Things Magdalene could never know, jokes held between the two of them, hopes and dreams and sorrows they'd shared with no one else save the departed Joseph. But then too the things she *had* been privy to—Imma's joy each time Jesus lived up to who He was. Each healing, each exorcism, each storm calmed.

His gaze moved at last, a small degree, to John. Dear young John. The only one of the Twelve still here.

He levered Himself again, wincing with the pain and effort. "Lady, there is your son. My friend—your mother."

Lips pressed tight, eyes watering, John nodded. He still had an arm around his own mother, but he reached his other one around Imma Mary too. "I will care for her," he swore, voice choked. "From this very hour until God takes one or the other of us home to Paradise."

Something relaxed in the Lord at that—was it relief, or was He simply growing too weak? He nodded. Swallowed. Whispered, "I thirst."

***

THREE YEARS EARLIER

Magdalene stood at the base of the road, staring up at the house on the hill. It had been four years since she'd last stood in this spot, with a very different group of people, though here for the same purpose. Their family had always spent the autumn and winter in Magdala, but they always came here, to their grand estate outside Jerusalem, in time for the Passover, which was now but a week away.

Four years ago, she hadn't paused at the base of the hill here, wondering what her reception would be when she climbed the road. She'd been with Abba, with Sarah, with Azur. They had been planning her sister's wedding as they walked, not realizing it would never happen. That Abba would be slain upon their return to Magdala. Four years ago, she had walked this road as a beloved daughter and sister.

Today she stood here as a stranger, one of a horde of pilgrims and disciples walking to Jerusalem for the Feast. Her feet had grown calloused, her heart tender. Hope had been nourished as she learned from Jesus, as she prayed for her family. They'd never returned her letter—but maybe, just maybe they would receive her anyway. Maybe they would forgive her. Maybe they would welcome her back as the father had his prodigal son in the parable Jesus had told.

Joanna and Khuza stopped beside her. Herod's family had journeyed to Jerusalem for the Passover too, so Khuza had been given permission to leave the palace as well. It wasn't the first time he and Joanna had been reunited, but it was the longest to date, and Magdalene saw the joy in her friend's eyes at his company. She had a feeling that after the Feast, Joanna would return to the palace with her husband, at least for a while. Magdalene couldn't begrudge her that.

"Don't be afraid, Mary."

She shouldn't be surprised at the voice, given that she spent every day seeking it out as much as possible. Still, it always surprised her when the Lord sought *her* out, when she looked over to find Him by her side.

She didn't bother putting on a smile she didn't feel. He would know it for a lie. Instead, she drew in a long breath and looked toward Azur's home again. "I want to repair this broken relationship. I want to introduce them to You, and for them not to refuse to listen just because I'm the one inviting them to, as Alexander did."

The Lord nodded along. "You are not responsible for whether they or anyone else opens their hearts to hear the Good News, Mary—you are only responsible for speaking it."

"I know." Even so, she couldn't quite rid her mind of that fear He told her not to embrace. What if they turned her away—but worse, what if it led them to turn *Him* away?

"Don't be afraid." He didn't have to speak the command again for it to echo in her mind.

Not a command exactly. More an…invitation. To put it into the hands of God and trust. Trust that He would meet these needs of her heart just as He had met every other need since she began traveling with Him.

Behind them, she could hear their group breaking up into smaller groups, some continuing toward the city, others moving into the fields to find places to rest for an hour or two and enjoy a meal from the food in their bags. Most of the crowds that had gathered and followed Him from place to place would fend for themselves now, seeking their own places to celebrate the Passover. Only Jesus and the Twelve, Imma Mary, the other Mary, Magdalene, Susanna, and Joanna and Khuza would be continuing together.

Where they would go depended entirely upon whether Azur and Sarah received her and offered their hospitality.

Even so, the Lord made no move to rush her. He simply stood there at her side, waiting for her to gather the courage, to rest in her trust.

If it were only for her own sake, perhaps she'd give in to the fear. Perhaps she would wallow in the loneliness that was the punishment she deserved for her sins.

That was selfish, though. Mending this bridge would serve the Lord today, but more, it could result in saving faith for her family. To refuse from fear to take this step was a sin as surely as the ones she'd committed at the palace.

With one last breath of a prayer for fortification, she strode forward, the eighteen friends she valued as family following in her wake but a few steps behind.

"Are you certain this is wise, Lord? We can go into the city and secure lodgings." Judas's doubt dripped from his every word. Doubt, as always, in her.

Magdalene pressed her lips together. If this group was truly her family now, then Judas was the elder brother she could never please, no matter what she tried.

She could only pray that Azur would be more forgiving.

As she neared the walled enclosure of the estate, the servants at the gate came to attention, both of them resting hands on their swords. "Who approaches?" one of them called out.

She searched her mind for the name that paired with the face and voice. "It is I, Moshe—Mary. I've just come from Magdala."

"My lady?" Moshe came forward a few steps to better see her, and his eyes widened. "Forgive me for not recognizing you at once. Eben, open the gate! The master's sister is here!"

Well, that was a good sign—he hadn't been instructed to bar the gates against her if ever she showed up. Magdalene breathed a little easier and glanced over at Jesus. He sent her an encouraging grin.

The gates swung open, and she led the way through them—if she was truly welcomed, then her traveling companions would be as well, she knew. Azur and Sarah had been taught well by Abba to always extend hospitality to sojourners, as long as they had means to do so.

Word moved more quickly than her feet. She could hear the cry going before her. "The master's sister has arrived! His younger sister!" Their voices all sounded joyful, excited.

The last doubt was removed when the front doors of the house flew open, and two figures burst from them at a run. She recognized her siblings even from this distance, and love swelled up in her chest.

She'd missed them. Until this moment, she hadn't realized how much she'd missed them.

At her side, Jesus chuckled. "What are you waiting for, My friend? *Go.*"

She went, taking off at a run, suddenly desperate to cover those last steps that she'd been dreading. Her headscarf flew off, but she paid it no mind. They were both calling her name, their arms open as they ran.

She met them halfway, laughter and tears joining hands as Azur scooped her into a hug and swung her around. The moment he put her feet back on the ground, Sarah was there too, her arms closing about them. She too had tears streaming down her cheeks but laughter in her throat.

"Mary! Finally, praise God. We have been praying you would come for Passover this year. Praying you were well."

"You cannot know our worry." Azur squeezed her tight, as if he never meant to let her go. "Why did you never write?"

"I did—six months ago. Did you not receive it?"

Her brother frowned. "No, we've had nothing from you, nor from Barnabas. Though we've heard the most horrible things from visitors who passed through Magdala—we were so afraid for you."

She held him back, even as she turned so press her forehead to her sister's. "It was likely all true—I lived many horrible things. But that was before I met John the Baptizer and then Jesus. Everything has changed now. Everything."

"The Teacher from Nazareth?" Azur finally loosened his grip a bit, though apparently only so he could see her face better. "We have heard about Him too—He has many of the religious leaders grumbling about blasphemy."

She shook her head and pulled away a bit, though she grabbed one of each of their hands. "He has never said a blasphemous word—He could not. But you needn't take my word for it. He is here, along with His disciples, His mother, and a few others."

"Here?" Azur's eyes lit, reminding her that, unlike Magdalene, he had always been at Abba's side whenever they hosted a teacher or scribe. "Excellent! We have a few others sharing the Feast with us too, of course, but we welcome your friends. I hope they can stay the whole week."

Magdalene nodded and wiped the tears from her cheeks. "With appreciation, yes. I know they'll want to venture frequently into the city, but I was hoping we—you—would offer your home."

"*Our* home." Azur narrowed his eyes playfully, tweaking her nose as he'd been doing since they were children. "You can't disown it just because the villa at Magdala has claimed your heart."

"And you know we're always happy to welcome more guests to the Feast." Sarah cupped Magdalene's cheek in one hand, using it to turn her face more fully her way so that she could send her gaze over every inch of it. "I have hungered for the sight of you. How is it that you've grown more beautiful with age?"

Magdalene laughed. She was certainly not what the women of the court would call beautiful these days—her skin was dark from the sun, her hair unadorned, her fine garments traded for more serviceable ones that could stand the rigors of travel. Had any of Herodias's women passed her on the street, they likely would have walked by without recognizing her.

And if they'd recognized her, they would have sniffed in disdain and crossed to the other side to avoid her.

Perhaps Sarah saw something else in Magdalene though— that she never intended to waste another moment trying to charm a man with her appearance or win the esteem of powerful women. Perhaps that contentment gave her features what no amount of oil or lotion or perfume ever could.

Sarah herself was as beautiful as ever too, but hers had *always* been the effortless sort. Her time had never been spent on her appearance, yet despite that, she always looked lovely and impeccable, unflustered by the mountain of tasks she took on every day. This was a perfect example—she didn't so much as bat an eye at a dozen and a half unexpected guests. If anything, she looked excited at the prospect of entertaining even more than she'd counted on.

Magdalene pulled her sister in for another embrace. "I've missed you. I cannot say how much I've missed you."

"We'll have plenty of time to catch up during the festival. But first…" Sarah turned them both back toward the gate and the group still meandering up the path to the house. "Perhaps you should introduce your friends?"

<hr>

Nothing was going according to plan. Magdalene stood in the doorway that connected the kitchen with the large dining hall, an amphora of wine in her hand, Sarah's instructions repeating in her head. Her feet had frozen in place, though, at the words whipping through the room like arrows.

"No!" The man who shouted it had taken to his feet too. She couldn't recall his name—her siblings had two dozen guests coming and going throughout the week, and they had blended together in her mind. Sadducees, including the high priest himself for one meal; Pharisees, from the houses of both Shammai and Hillel. Scribes from every different order and sect.

It was no wonder that conversations had turned argumentative more than once—questioning and debating was in fact one of the favorite methods of the Pharisees for discerning truth. She had listened far more attentively than she would have done before her months with Jesus, trying to identify when each speaker departed from God's view and followed his own logic instead. She had found the conversations riveting, especially when Jesus weighed in with the wisdom and insight she'd come to expect of Him.

She just hadn't expected the guests to begin debating *her.*

The man sliced a hand through the air. "She is a sinner. You know the Law, Azur—to dine with a sinner is to make oneself unclean. That you would even permit that harlot into your house—"

"Do not speak that way of my sister." Azur stood too, his cheeks as red as Magdalene's felt. "She is no harlot."

"She is *worse!* She sinned not for money to survive but for the pure pleasure of it!" The man spat—actually spat—upon Sarah's immaculate tiled floor.

Jesus set His chalice down with a quiet click. "Which is worse, friend—the man who borrows one large sum of money and puts off his creditors for years but then finally pays the money back in full, or the man who borrows a little every day until his debts cannot be counted but who continually insists he needn't pay anything back because each withdrawal was small?"

The man spun on Him. "What is that supposed to mean?"

"Mary sinned. She has admitted it, repented of it, and turned from it. It has been forgiven, despite the sin being great." He lifted His brows. "You have committed no murder, no adultery, you have never stolen your neighbor's livestock.

But are you without sin? Have you never spoken a harsh word against your father? Have you never turned a blind eye to the poor in the street, whom God commanded you to care for? Have you never given to men the regard you should reserve only for God?"

The man's face mottled.

Jesus gave him the exact look Abba had always given them when he wanted them to learn something for their own good. "My friend, in the eyes of God, hating your neighbor is as grave as killing him. Looking after a woman with lust is tantamount to taking her to your bed. Intention matters to God every bit as much as action."

The man's eyes bulged. "Then no one is without sin!"

"Ah, he's hit upon the truth at last." Jesus laughed and reclined against His cushion. "Exactly my point. No one, man or woman, is without sin. So I ask you again—which is worse? To recognize one's great fault and repent of it, or to refuse to see one's many smaller sins and so never change?"

For a moment, she thought the words had hit their mark. The man stood utterly still, his gaze on Jesus as he no doubt wrestled with the choice the Lord put before him—repent and forgive or stand before God with only his own tarnished righteousness to commend him.

She had seen countless people stand like that over the last six months. Some now followed the Lord wherever He journeyed, others followed His teachings in their own homes and towns. Others turned and walked away as Alexander had. Unchanged?

No. She couldn't believe that. One could not encounter the Lord without being changed. It was just that if one denied His call to something better, then one in fact chose something so much worse. If one chose not to be His friend, one became His enemy.

Gripping the amphora of wine that Sarah had sent her to refill, she prayed silently that this stranger would choose the path that led to light and life and eternity.

Instead, he turned on his heel. "I will not sit in a house with that woman and be sullied by her mere proximity. I will not do business any longer, Azur, with a man who would continue to claim such a wretch as his sister. And you can be certain, Teacher, that I will report to the Sanhedrin what sort of rabble *You* associate with too, and what lies You speak about the very nature of God. How dare You insinuate that someone like her would ever be welcome in His presence?"

This last he aimed over his shoulder as he stalked from the room.

Jesus sighed. Azur winced at the slam of the door that rang throughout the house. Magdalene set the wine down and hurried forward, falling to her knees at the Master's feet. "I am sorry, Lord. I am so sorry."

This time, Jesus urged her up instead of letting her say anything more. "You may be filled with sorrow on his behalf, Mary—but you cannot be sorry. You've done nothing wrong."

She lifted her face toward His, knowing her incredulity was painted upon her own. "How can You say that? You know what I've done! That my sins would now cause You trouble—"

"Mary, stop." He actually laughed as He spoke. "Those who haven't the ears to hear or the eyes to see will have no shortage of complaints against Me—and you will certainly not be the only company of Mine they object to."

"But…"

"How far is the east from the west, Mary?"

"What?" She leaned back on her heels, her brows pulled together in a way they did frequently these days as she tried to wrap her mind and heart around all He said. "I…I don't know, Lord."

"You don't know because no one does—it cannot be measured. There is no east-most point, no west-most, unlike north and south. When the Father promises to remove your sins as far as the east is from the west, He was not just speaking poetically—He was promising something profound. You cannot be further from your sins than you are now, after He forgave them. Unless you think He offers a half-hearted forgiveness?"

She shook her head. "No. What God cleans is whiter than snow. The sins are washed away." That was another image they had explored as they walked, why John and the Twelve baptized in living, flowing water—to remind the penitents that the sins were washed away once and for all.

They were new creations. Spotless, unblemished.

Her eyes fell shut. "Forgive me. Not for his accusations but for forgetting for even a moment that I am a new creature now."

"I will remind you whenever you need it."

She smiled, knowing He would do just that. And knowing she would need it again—because as kind as His eyes were as they looked upon her, several sets of eyes around the table shot rebukes at her even now. Some for what she'd done, no doubt—but she suspected a few were because she sat at the Teacher's feet even now.

And Judas—she was beginning to lose hope that he would ever look at her any other way.

CHAPTER TWELVE

R obbery."

"They are liars and cheats, that's what."

"Blemished, they said—so they could sell me one of their own at an inflated price!"

Magdalene stuck close to her sister's side as they navigated through Jerusalem the day before Passover, not relishing finding herself caught in the middle of any of the squabbling, outraged pilgrims. The city was bursting with Jews from all over the world, and it seemed most of them were angry today.

"What are they upset about?" she whispered to her sister, eying one particularly volatile giant of a man who was storming away from the Temple, shouting in Greek.

Sarah sighed and linked their arms together. "It's like this every Passover. People bring their own lambs for the sacrifice, but they're always refused and told they're blemished, that they must purchase one of the Temple lambs."

Magdalene frowned. "All of them? Perhaps a few have blemishes, but do they think that shepherds from the country cannot tell a sound lamb from a flawed one?"

"Oh, they can tell." Sarah's voice sounded weary as she led them around another cluster of disgruntled travelers. "Just as they can tell a swindle when they see one. The Temple lambs are five times the price they should be, but the pilgrims are offered no recourse. They either purchase one or they cannot celebrate the Feast they came here for."

"That isn't right." She looked around her at the thousands of people who had come to Jerusalem to celebrate the faithfulness of God, only to be smacked in the face with the greed of men.

"It's worse. They won't accept any foreign coins either, so they must first change their money. At a steep fee, of course."

No wonder there was so much grumbling. Magdalene shook her head and wrinkled her nose against the smells that accosted her when they rounded another corner. She was far from the pampered palace dweller she'd been last year at this time, well acquainted with the scents of hard work and travel and animals. But when they were moving through the country-side, there were never quite this many people in this amount of space, all with bleating lambs and braying donkeys and cages of doves flapping their demand for release, children crying and parents complaining.

She found herself looking forward to finishing their business in the city and making the two-mile trek back to their house, away from all the commotion.

A huge roar of sound stopped them in their tracks a minute later, louder even than the general din she'd been bemoaning. Animals in distress, crashing, shouts going up—had a house collapsed or something near the Temple?

She and Sarah exchanged a look and ran to join the other bystanders eager to see what was going on. They ended up pressed from all sides, barely getting a view of the outer court of the Temple.

She got enough of a glimpse, though, for her jaw to drop. Jesus stood in the center of overturned tables, a whip made of cord in His hand as He shouted. "You have made My Father's house into a den of thieves! Clear all this out!"

All around Him, cattle and sheep ran away from the ruckus, out of the Temple courts—to a new roar of applause and shouting from the onlookers.

"It's high time someone takes a stand!" someone yelled from Magdalene's left.

"A champion of the people!" came from behind.

"It's Jesus—the Teacher from Nazareth!" someone else added.

Sarah dug her fingers into Magdalene's arm and pulled her away, out of the crush of bodies, not letting go even after they'd broken free of the mob. Her hand shook. "Mary, who is this man? He is inviting all manner of trouble with such actions!"

Perhaps she shouldn't have chuckled—it only earned her a sharp look from her older sister. She couldn't help it though. "That's the question we all ask, Sarah. The question we all must answer. I am happy to tell you all I've learned, to share all I've seen, but ultimately you must decide for yourself what you believe about Him."

Sarah sent a wary look over her shoulder and slipped her hand through the crook of Magdalene's elbow. "I admit His teaching stirs something within me, and it reaffirms all Abba taught us. But to take a stand like *that*? He'll have made power-ful enemies with that one rash move."

"It wasn't rash. He is many things—bold and capable of the impossible. But He does nothing without thought or purpose."

Though they were weaving through the packed marketplace, Sarah didn't take her eyes from Magdalene's face. "He really cast…demons out of you?"

She'd already poured out her personal tale to Sarah and Azur, everything from the pit she had sunk into through her deliverance from it. Had they believed her? Enough to welcome her home, enough to believe she'd sinned and repented. But perhaps granting that their sister had indeed been in the thrall of demons was too difficult to believe without having first seen it.

Magdalene pointed at the stall they'd come into the city for, the spice dealers from Egypt. "He did. And He has performed many more miracles since then. He heals any who come to Him, whatever their infirmity."

So often in their childhood, Sarah and Magdalene had been at odds—bickering over toys and attention, and holding opposite opinions on just about everything, often simply for the sake of it. But this was one thing she prayed they could agree on. Because this one thing mattered more than any other.

Sarah drew them to a halt a step away from the spice merchant's table, looking deep into Magdalene's eyes. "I'm glad. Glad He healed you. Glad He returned you to us. Will you stay for a while after the Feast? To tell us about your travels with the Teacher?"

Magdalene opened her mouth, but she had no idea what words to offer her sister. She didn't know what the Master's plans were after Passover—would He want to stay in Jerusalem for a while? Or at least stay in the region? If so, He might agree to use their family's home as a base. Then again, He could just as easily decide it was time to travel somewhere else entirely.

She'd never even considered staying behind when He left, not until this very moment, looking into her sister's eyes. She'd seen Sarah in the throes of every possible emotion over the years, just as Sarah had seen her. But she couldn't ever recall seeing such longing in her eyes.

Was it Magdalene's company she craved—or the teachings of Jesus?

Magdalene reached over to rest her free hand on the arm looped around hers. "I want you to believe in Him as I do. I want you to grasp hold of the life He offers."

"I want that too. When you fell at His feet the other night—I have never seen such adoration as was on your face. He must be more than the average rabbi to inspire that in you."

It nearly made her laugh. "Much more. So much more."

Her sister's brows pinched together. "Are you…in love with Him?"

Now she *did* laugh and pulled her sister forward again. "If you mean romantically, I cannot even imagine it." She shook her head to punctuate the absurdity. Romantic love was all about the rush of feeling, the delight of thinking of the other, the desire to possess and be possessed by them.

The very thought turned her stomach. She had sought that where she shouldn't have. She had given what could never be restored. She had put all her hopes in a very mortal man and had her heart dashed on the cruel rocks of reality. All because she had thought that life would not be worth living if she didn't find a husband to love her, to validate her, to desire her.

"This is a very different sort of love, Sarah. I haven't even words to describe it." She closed her eyes to search for one, and her nose caught the scents of the many spices now before her. Her skin soaked up the sunshine that reflected off the white stone buildings. Her ears heard the chaos of life. "He shone light into my darkness. He restored my soul. I would follow Him anywhere, just to see what He does next, to hear His words. I love Him in a way I've never loved anyone—and yet in a way that challenges me to love everyone."

"Well," said a new voice from behind them, masculine and cold. "I'm so glad to hear you've found someone to make you happy."

She spun around, both surprised and not to see Alexander looming over her. Of course he would have come to Jerusalem for Passover, but why did he have to find her in the throngs? Why could they not have missed each other? And if they must pass, why in that moment, when he clearly heard only part of what she said?

She sighed, weariness settling on her shoulders. "Alexander, good day." She motioned to Sarah, who'd turned too and stared with wide eyes at their unexpected eavesdropper, whose name she'd already heard. "Allow me to introduce my sister, Sarah."

Alexander flicked a glance at Sarah, offered a tight, polite smile. "How good to meet you." Back to Magdalene. "Are you betrothed then? To that nobody from Nazareth?"

As if Jesus would ever take a wife, when His mission was to serve as many people as He could! "Of course not. I am merely one of His many disciples."

"Are you?" Thunder darkened Alexander's brows. "I hear you have been traveling with Him all these months."

"Along with many other women, yes. Joanna and I have been in the company of His mother, several other ladies from Galilee, and the mothers of a few other disciples." She tried not to prickle at the implications in his words, but prickle she did.

"And He is now enjoying Passover at your brother's home."

It was a statement, not a question, so she saw no need to respond to it. "Do you wish to hear Him teach? You are welcome to join us one evening—"

"And mark myself as a pariah in the eyes of the religious leaders?" He snorted. "No thank you. Anyone associated with Him after that little display of His in the Temple a few minutes ago will regret it."

His posture, the look in his eyes begged her to ask what he was talking about, and no doubt he had his own unfavorable explanation of what had just transpired. Magdalene wasn't about to indulge him. "If ever you change your mind, you are welcome."

A flash of disappointment, one of frustration, then that ice settled back in his eyes again. "Khuza and I were in the same caravan. He said Joanna is returning with him after the Feast. I suppose that means you'll be returning to Magdala too."

Did he *want* her to? Or was he rather hoping for a contradiction, so they could avoid any more moments like this? Regardless of his reasoning, her answer was still a shake of her head. "I don't imagine so. I will either continue with the Teacher or stay with my siblings for a while." Whichever the Lord advised.

"You will do whatever you please, as you always do." Eyes glinting with bitterness, he turned and stalked away.

Magdalene sighed and leaned into her sister. "Talk about poor timing."

"He must have cared for you a great deal." Sarah had turned a bit to watch him melt into the crowd. "That means there is yet hope for reconciliation. I remember Abba speaking of his family, of his respect for them."

"Reconciliation?" Her incredulity saturated her tone, she knew. "If you mean that perhaps someday he will forgive me, then I pray you are right. But beyond that…no."

Sarah sent her an exasperated look. "Why not? He is a handsome man, upstanding, and I am quite certain he wouldn't be acting like that if you hadn't won a special place in his heart. You are too young, Mary, to give up all hope of a husband and family."

A breath of laughter escaped as she searched the stall for the spices they needed—nutmeg, cardamom, saffron. "This, coming from you!"

"It isn't the same. I was betrothed. I am a widow, I have that dignity, even if I have no son to care for me. Azur has promised me a place in his home forever, and that will be enough."

But what did Magdalene have? That was the question her sister didn't exactly put to words, though it clamored in the air between them nonetheless.

Sarah was smiling at the merchant. "Good morning, Vaak."

The Egyptian gave her a wide smile made distinctive by a chipped front tooth. "Good morning, Mistress Sarah. Back again so soon for my fine spices?"

"We have more guests for the Feast than I had dared to hope. I need more nutmeg, saffron, and cardamom—the same amount as last week, please."

"Of course, mistress. And for you, I will even give you the same price." He winked. "Though for everyone else, prices have doubled this week, yes?"

Sarah laughed. "You are too good to me. And allow me to introduce my sister, Mary—everyone calls her Magdalene these days, as she runs our family estate in Magdala."

The Egyptian tipped his head to her, his gaze intense as he seemed to memorize every feature. "Mary Magdalene. I will remember. And give you the same prices your sister haggled from me long ago, yes?"

She forced her lips into a smile. It wasn't his fault she felt the old bristling that Sarah had always managed to elicit from her like no one else. "Thank you, Vaak. I am not in Jerusalem often, but I will be certain to seek out you above all other spice traders whenever I am."

"My caravans go elsewhere too. Magdala—near the court of Herod, yes? I have long been trying to gain space in those markets." He lifted a brow as he measured nutmeg into a pouch on a scale.

Her gaze roamed over his offerings. Pots and jars filled with every spice imaginable, for cooking and medicine and embalming, even. "If you are my sister's choice, then I know your spices must be the best. I would be happy to send a letter of introduction to my steward, Barnabas, who can no doubt assist you with that."

His smile flashed again, showing shockingly white, even teeth, and his booming laugh joined the din of the street. "I knew I liked your family! Just tell no one the deal I give you, yes?"

She smiled her own assurances, waited while he chatted with her sister and finished his measuring, watched Sarah dole out the coins, and then tucked the small bags into her larger one. All the while trying to determine why her sister's words had pricked her so.

"I do not need a husband," she said at last, softly, as they walked away.

"What then, you will just live alone at the villa for the rest of your days?" Sarah made a noise in the back of her throat. "What a fulfilling life."

"Will I have to? Will Azur not welcome *me* into his home if I choose not to wed?"

Sarah looked genuinely baffled. "I'm certain he would—but since when would you want him to? You always made it abundantly clear that you were destined for greater things."

Had she? That Magdalene seemed so far removed, in some ways. She had vague recollections of the ambitions and dreams of the headstrong girl she'd once been, but trying to remember them was akin to trying to piece together a dream days after waking from it. She had only fleeting images, impressions, snippets of what had once fueled her.

What a horrible sister she must have been. The weight of that bowed her head. "I am sorry, Sarah. I will make no excuses for who I once was. I will simply assure you that the only thing I'm interested in pursuing now is righteousness that will lead to eternal life."

Her sister stared at her for a long moment. And though she then shook her head, it was with a smile.

Darkness was falling by the time Magdalene managed to find a moment when she could speak privately with Jesus. The whole group had enjoyed a wonderful meal together, and afterward the Lord had slipped away in that way that He often did, when He waved the disciples on to their own pursuits. Her Rabboni, she knew, would take the chance for solitary prayer—and she would not interrupt that precious time He took with His Father.

She would simply ask Him for a slip of time while He was on His way to that prayer. It meant leaving Sarah to supervise the cleanup from the meal, but she would return soon. For now, she hurried after the Teacher, not surprised anymore when He held up at the edge of Azur's garden, obviously waiting for her.

He always knew when she was coming. And He always greeted her with a smile. "You have much on your heart, My friend," He said, turning onto one of the paths through the garden.

Magdalene nodded. "My siblings—they have expressed interest in having me stay beyond the Feast. They want to hear about my travels with You."

Jesus kept smiling, nodding along with her. "I am certainly not surprised that your family wishes to spend time with you."

He offered nothing else—no judgment, no encouragement. She blustered out a breath. "I don't know what I should do. I want them to learn all they possibly can of You, and of who I've become. But I don't want to turn back from following You, Lord."

His chuckle blended with the night birds tweeting their hellos to the moon. "Mary, there are many who say they wish to follow Me but are always looking for an excuse as to why they can't come yet, or why I cannot expect much from them. To them, I say that if they are not willing to give up the thing keeping them from Me, they are not worthy to follow at all. But this is not your dilemma. You *do* follow. Whether you are in the camp or in the court or with your family, you still follow Me. That is what matters." He paused, reached out, and clapped a hand to her shoulder. "Telling them all you've seen is no shirking of that path. It is part of it. This will bring glory to God. This will equip your family to believe."

It would? That brought not just relief, but joy. "Then I will stay for a while. To share with them. But I want to rejoin You soon—perhaps You'll pass this way again in a few weeks?"

The moonlight caught on His teeth and made them gleam. "We will indeed. You can rest easy on that score. Now..."

"Right." She backed up a step. "You'll want Your privacy for Your time of prayer."

"I will. Although first..." He nodded toward the garden wall, where the shadows were deeper. "I believe our new friend Nicodemus has some questions. If you'll excuse Me?"

Nicodemus…it took her a moment to pair the name with one of the well-respected Pharisees her brother had invited to share the Feast with them. Unlike the one who had stormed out days ago, this man had been listening intently to all that Jesus said, as had the one called Joseph—a name that had made Jesus and His mother smile—from Arimathea. She smiled, a prayer in her heart that this new friend would become a lasting one for her Lord.

"Of course, Rabboni. Thank You." Feeling light as the breeze, Magdalene returned to the house.

CHAPTER THIRTEEN

"How is this His kingdom?"

"What?" Magdalene tore her gaze away from Jesus as He drank from the sponge soaked with sour wine and looked over at John, who stared at the Lord with a furrowed brow.

The disciple gave a slow shake of his head. "He said…last night. At the Feast. He shared the Third Cup with us, the Cup of Blessing, and said the strangest thing about it being His blood poured out for us. He called the bread His body. But then He called a halt to the Feast before we could finish with the Fourth Cup."

Magdalene frowned too, even though that explained why she hadn't been able to find them in the upper room when the ceremony should have still been underway. Why Judas was out about his evil business. "Where did you all go?"

"Gethsemane." John rubbed his eyes. He looked tired, so tired.

"But…why? He always enjoyed Passover so deeply, why would He end the Feast too soon?" It was unheard of, certainly by the Lord. The Fourth Cup had always been His favorite part—the Cup of Redemption. Every time they'd taken the meal together, she had marveled at the light, the joy in His eyes when they arrived at that final portion of the service, when they remembered how God had delivered their people.

John shook his head. "I don't know. When we asked about that final cup, He…He said He would not drink wine again until He came into His kingdom." With a flair of his nostrils, he motioned toward the cross. "How is *that* His kingdom? How?"

She could only mirror the shake of his head. It made no sense—but why should it? Nothing about this day made sense. Jesus, her Lord and Savior, should not be hanging on a cross. His precious mother should not be sinking even now to her knees, as if the last bit of her energy had just seeped into the ground. The Twelve should not have all scattered. The crowds that had sung out "Hosanna to the Son of David" just a week ago should not now be ridiculing and mocking the One they'd begged to save them.

The skies were unnaturally dark, though no clouds blocked the sun. An eclipse? Perhaps…but there was more to it than that. As Magdalene searched the heavens with her gaze, she sensed again those once-familiar forces converging. "Please, Father God." But though she prayed the words, she didn't even know what she was asking, or why she bothered. If Jesus, whom God always heard with such clarity, could not stop this, then how could she?

On the cross, her Lord cried out, a sound so filled with pain that it ripped at her own soul and made Imma double over. The silence that fell in the wake of that cry pressed hard upon her, but then He dragged in one more breath and whispered, "It is finished."

His head—that thorn-pierced, blood-streaked, light-bearing head—hung down.

The darkness converged. The earth…the earth shook beneath her feet, bringing Magdalene to her knees along with everyone else on the hillside. All of nature, it seemed, was rent in two, the screams of all the onlookers just background noise to the din Magdalene heard from the skies. She clapped her hands over her ears, but still she heard those horrible screeches from the enemies Jesus had banished from her soul three years ago.

"He's gone," Imma whispered, head bowed to the trembling earth. "He's gone."

"Come." John's voice sounded strange, strangled. "We should get away from this place."

Magdalene shook her head, her gaze fixed again on Jesus. "No. I'm not going anywhere." It wasn't too late, was it? He could still…He could…

"Nor am I," Imma Mary insisted. "I will hold Him when they take Him down. My precious Son."

Vaguely she heard the chief priests giving instructions for the convicts' legs to be broken to hurry their deaths along before Sabbath came. Vaguely she saw one of the centurions shake his head as he approached Jesus, declaring Him already dead.

Already dead.

"No." She dug her fingers into the packed soil beneath her. It felt real enough—the grit packed itself under her fingernails, the small stones bit into her fingertips, the sharp smell of dirt and blood stung her nostrils. And yet how could it be?

Her eyes slid shut for two beats, three. This would be it, then. The End of the Ages that the Lord had spoken of. He'd warned them all that destruction would come, didn't He? This must be the first stage. First, the Son of God gave up His life. The earth shook its protest. Next fire would surely rain down from heaven, the city would be swallowed up, devastation would tear them all apart.

The Light had left the world. What could possibly happen now, but for all of creation to be consumed by darkness?

The soldiers took Jesus's limp form down from the cross and made no objection when Imma Mary reached out to cradle Him in her arms, keening. Magdalene averted her eyes to give Imma a moment of privacy with His body.

She didn't know how long they stayed there, the Lord's mother weeping over Him. But at last, John urged her up. The other Mary murmured to her son, "Get her home, help her rest. Magdalene and I will see where they…where they bury Him."

Bury Him. Magdalene's eyes burned, and she felt the shaking in her soul, even though the earth had stilled. They couldn't bury Him. He couldn't be dead. The enemy couldn't have won. She would wake up and find it all a bad dream, that was all. A nightmare.

John's mother slid an arm around Magdalene and pulled her to her feet. "Up, my child. Up. We must see what happens to His body so we can tell the others."

Magdalene nodded as she scurried back onto her feet, dusting her hands off on her clothes. This might be the last thing she was ever able to do for Him—and so she would do it with all her heart. She would follow Him to whatever grave He was given. She would anoint His body.

And then…she didn't know. She didn't know what other action she could ever take. What would have any meaning after this?

"Magdalene?"

She spun at the voice, not able to place to whom it belonged until she saw the figure striding up the hill. Joseph of Arimathea. He was on the council, and she could tell from the weary lines of his face that he had spent countless hours over the last several days trying in vain to put a stop to these horrible proceedings. "Joseph."

His gaze had gone past her, to the crosses. Sorrow blanketed him. "I'm too late. I was…I was making arrangements. For a tomb. Still, I'd hoped that I would make it here before…"

Before the world came to an end. Magdalene gripped the other Mary's hand tight in hers. "A tomb?"

Joseph's gaze drifted back to her. He nodded. "I have a new one I purchased recently. No one has ever been laid in it. When I heard the pronouncement against Him, I went immediately to Pilate to ask for His body." His voice broke. "If I can do nothing else, at least I can do this. I can see to it that He has an honorable burial."

The other Mary sniffed. "Did he agree?"

"He did, praise God, though the council protested and said a convicted criminal should not receive such a thing. Pilate overruled them."

"Good," Mary said, relief in her tone. "Good."

Magdalene watched as they dismantled the Lord's cross. There was nothing *good* about this day. Nothing.

Joseph cleared his throat. "I spoke with Nicodemus too—he is arranging for the ointments and spices and aloes. He will bring them to the tomb, but..."

He looked to the sky, and Magdalene did too. The strange darkness was beginning to fade, but that only meant it made way for true evening. "There isn't enough time. Before Sabbath descends."

After everything else, that shouldn't have made tears clog her throat. But it wasn't right that the heavenly Prince should be laid in a tomb without even the proper dressing. He should have been given every honor, every attention. They should spend hours preparing His body.

And they would—*she* would. Perhaps not this evening, as she'd like—if they defied the Sabbath for His sake, she could only imagine the consequences. But at first light on the first day of the week, she would be there, at the tomb.

All the powers of darkness couldn't keep her away.

EIGHTEEN MONTHS EARLIER, MAGDALA

Magdalene inhaled deeply, her smile blooming as the rich scents wafted up from the dish before her. "This smells amazing. Rhoda has been using Vaak's spices exclusively, you say?"

Barnabas rolled a hand toward the window and the village beyond it. "Indeed. And as you've instructed, we've been sharing the meals with the poor, and word has then spread about the fine ingredients, and other leading families have inquired as to our source for them. His hold on the market is sound now."

"And the poor are being fed, which is even more important." Magdalene sampled the bread-and-meat creation and nearly groaned as the flavors exploded in her mouth. She had traveled through much of Israel over the last year and a half, had eaten meals cooked over campfires, meals prepared by the wealthiest families, and everything in between. She had enjoyed feasts and festivals at her brother's table with joy in her heart.

But no one the world over could cook quite like Barnabas's wife here in Magdala. "It is good to be home for a little while."

"Rhoda is pleased to have the promise of dinners hosted here this month and is especially excited to both hear Jesus for herself and also get to take care of your brother and sister again."

Magdalene was happy about that herself. Especially since her reason for spending a whole month in Magdala, despite the fact that Jesus only planned to be in the area for a week or so, would involve something she hadn't been certain she'd ever do again.

Go to the palace.

Even thinking of it made her stomach knot and twist. She hadn't set foot in those halls since she fled them the day that Alexander broke things off and John the Baptizer's head was brought in on a silver platter. She had never really even looked back, not at the life, not at the shadows she'd escaped, not at everything it represented.

But she missed Joanna when her friend was back here in Galilee. And she missed Salome, having only seen her once, here in her villa, for a few hours. They'd exchanged letters, but it wasn't the same.

And now her young friend's betrothal was coming to an end—she had enjoyed the standard year of preparation for her royal nuptials, and a few extra months besides, thanks to her bridegroom having been traveling abroad. Now, though, the time had come for the wedding, and Magdalene had been humbled to receive an invitation to be one of Salome's maidens.

Before she'd left court perhaps she had taken for granted that she'd be among the number of unmarried women preparing the bride for her bridegroom and participating in the ceremony. But now? She had assumed that when she left court, she forfeited that position to one of the other scores of young women eager to step in.

Salome had been adamant though. She'd come to see Magdalene here the last time she'd come through the area, and she'd embraced her and declared her one of her few true friends.

Tears had surged then, and they pricked her eyes again now at the memory. So many things from that part of her life were a smudge of nightmarish memory. So many things she was ashamed of, so many things she wanted to run from and never look back at but to praise God for how far He'd lifted her from that mire.

But Salome and Joanna were two of the shining lights that pierced that darkness, and if somehow Magdalene had managed to be a true friend, then it was surely testament to the grace of God. And she would honor that with gratitude by standing with her friend now.

Even so, she dreaded actually leaving for the palace and having to stay there for a week. If anything were to test this new person she'd become, it would be revisiting that world.

But it would help to know that Sarah and Azur were right here. That Joanna, also a new creature, would be beside her with Khuza. That Barnabas and Rhoda would be praying for her every day too. And that they had goals well beyond the wedding feasts. Plans to live up to Abba's reputation and Azur's practice in Judea and make this house once again a center for discussion of things true and beautiful and good.

"Magdalene?"

At Joanna's voice, Magdalene finished off the last few bites of her breakfast and rose from the table. "In here!" To Barnabas she said, "Tell Rhoda that I haven't tasted anything so good in half a year or more."

Her steward grinned. "You do know how to make her glow with pride and pleasure, my lady. I will deliver the message. And I will have the rest of the reports ready to go over with you after the wedding."

"Good. Azur will join us too." The words came more easily than she'd honestly expected them to. Before she met Jesus, she had been so adamant about being able to run this villa by herself that she never would have invited her brother to join her in a meeting with Barnabas.

But she had nothing to prove and could only gain from her brother's wisdom. Besides, she and Azur had enjoyed numerous sessions planning how to use their resources for the kingdom of heaven, in ways befitting Jesus's teaching, and had implemented several of their ideas both here and at his estate. She was eager to have a conversation along the same lines with Barnabas.

Joanna entered the room with a smile both bright and tired. She had a hand bracing the small of her back, which only served to accentuate the enormous round of her stomach. Magdalene rose with a grin. "Please tell me you didn't walk from the palace."

Her friend chuckled. "If I had tried it, I would be a long ways off yet. 'Quick' is not a word used to describe me these days."

Magdalene gave her cheek a kiss of greeting and touched a hand to her friend's stomach when a little foot or elbow or hand made a bump move in an arc. She couldn't help but laugh. "This little one is clearly ready to make his appearance."

Joanna rubbed the spot, wincing. "And we are ready for him to. But this is the real question of the day: Are you ready to come to the palace?"

Was she? No. But since Joanna and Khuza had been kind enough to send a wagon—and a very-expectant Joanna—for her, she certainly wasn't going to refuse. "Of course. And thank you again for accompanying me. I confess I feel a bit like I imagine Hananiah, Mishael, and Azariah must have felt when they faced the fiery furnace in Babylon."

"Understandable." Joanna linked their arms together and aimed them for the door. "But one thing I've found is that, when you are viewing the world through the eyes that Jesus has taught us to use, you can find many opportunities to do the work of God, even in Herod's palace."

"I have no doubt of that. I suppose I am simply…afraid. That my eyes are not that good. Or rather, that they will be blinded by the old shadows if I go there again."

"Never." Joanna bumped their shoulders together. "You are not subject to those forces anymore. You are free. You have been made new."

"I know." And when she was in the presence of the Lord, she couldn't forget that. But when apart from Him? The fears could crowd in so quickly if she didn't keep her eyes firmly focused on her Savior.

She would simply have to remember what He'd told her after her first separation from the group—that as long as she was doing His work, she was following Him, wherever she was. And really, who needed to hear of the life-giving water He offered more than those in the court?

Prayer would strengthen her, and part of her prayer was that God would show her how to do His will in her week at the palace, that He would soften hearts and open ears to the message of repentance and salvation.

"You're right. I'm ready." The Lord would make her so. She and Joanna went to tell Sarah and Azur farewell, and then, after fortifying hugs from her siblings, she went outside to see that her things had been loaded into Khuza's ornate wagon.

She ran a self-conscious hand over her headscarf, down her tunic. Traveling with Imma Mary and her company, she rarely gave any thought to her appearance. But to be part of Salome's wedding, she would have to trade in the clothes that had become worn and familiar and put on the ones provided by Herod. She would have to uncover her hair again.

She would soon look very much like the old Magdalene—though she knew that the other ladies would be snickering behind their hands at her now-callused palms and sun-darkened face. Magdalene, beauty of the court, was long gone. And she wouldn't have it any other way.

Joanna's servants helped her into the wagon, and Magdalene climbed up with a smile of thanks for the hand that the eunuch offered her. Soon they were rattling along the road, and Joanna was regaling her with all the plans she and Khuza had been making for their little one. Another reason Magdalene had decided to spend a month in Magdala—she wanted to be on hand to help her best friend in those first weeks of motherhood. Not that she knew the first thing about babes, but she and Sarah both wanted to do whatever they could to help.

As they neared the town, the wagon slowed, and Magdalene peered out to see why. As expected, they were passing another group of travelers—weary-looking ones who bore the marks of a long journey.

"Oh no." Joanna surveyed them with concern, gripping Magdalene's hand. "Those are some of Alexander's people. It doesn't look as though their trip went well—they should have been returning with a caravan two or three times that size."

Another mention that made her stomach clench. "Perhaps they were simply separated from the larger group."

"Perhaps." Her tone, however, didn't speak of hope. "I certainly pray it is so, for his family's sake. The villa has not been doing well. The previous owners had not given the land its sabbath rest for many years, and the crops are paying the price."

Magdalene sighed. Very few people actually gave their fields the rest that the Lord had ordered for them every seven years—whether from greed or lack of trust in God's provision. But Abba, and his abba before him, had always observed the sabbath year meticulously in all their property, and God had rewarded them with bountiful yields in the other six years, with more than enough surplus to make up for that seventh year of rest.

For his family's sake. Did Joanna mean the family—brother and father and younger sisters—in Cyrene, or…? "Has he married yet?" Magdalene kept Alexander in her daily prayers, but she rarely asked for an update on him. Somehow it seemed awkward even to discuss him, knowing how angry he'd been with her.

Joanna shrugged. "There is always talk of him entering into negotiations with some family or another, but it has never been more than gossip. His official stance has historically been that he wants to get the new estate on firmer footing before he takes a wife. But if you ask me…"

Magdalene felt her friend's gaze rest heavily on her, though she was still watching the small caravan trudge by. "Don't say it, Joanna. We only knew each other three weeks. He cannot possibly still be pining for me."

"I don't think it just *you* he's pining for. But you, *Magdalene,* are far more than just yourself to a potential husband, as well you know."

Her villa. All the wealth Abba had left her. Of course. Perhaps if one were thinking only of romance and love, that didn't shine a favorable light on Alexander, but it was a very practical consideration. He had come here not only to find and marry the girl his father had chosen for him, but to marry into her property. In his eyes, she'd cheated him of that, and the investment he'd made instead wasn't going so well for him, it seemed.

She sighed and faced forward again. Joanna was right. No doubt he'd have shrugged off their acquaintance long before now if it were a simple matter of romantic disappointment. But in his eyes, she'd cheated him of his future. And that was much more difficult to forgive.

CHAPTER FOURTEEN

The music was all wrong. It was too loud, too many instruments, the wrong kind of instruments. Instead of providing a beautiful backdrop to songs of praise, as she'd grown accustomed to, this music raced and spun and asked the listeners to abandon themselves to something far different from worship.

It made her heart race, but not with the giddy abandon that the other revelers seemed to be enjoying—the revelry that she vaguely remembered experiencing herself in the days of palace life. Magdalene rubbed a hand over her chest, willing the band of anxiety to ease. She hadn't felt this way in months, even years at this point, but returning here reminded her of all the things she'd escaped. All the reasons for escaping it.

But I am not my own. I am not of the darkness anymore either. I belong to the Light, to the Dayspring, to the Lord Most High. Standing against the wall, well out of the way of the dancers, Magdalene closed her eyes and drew in a perfume-laden breath and prayed as Jesus had taught them. *Father in heaven, Your very name is holy and to be revered. Let Your kingdom come to fruition here on earth, Your will be done in our lives and here in Herod's court, just as it is accomplished in the heavenly courts....*

"It's awfully loud, isn't it?"

Magdalene opened her eyes again at the soft, feminine voice, and found a young woman she'd never met standing close to her side, surveying the crowds of royal guests with obvious unease. She wore provided wedding garments like everyone else, but she'd kept the light, wispy headcloth of a modest Jewess over her hair. Magdalene wished she'd been able to do the same, but given her status as one of Salome's maidens, that hadn't been an option for her. She'd had to dress like the others.

For her new companion, she produced a smile. "It is. I cannot believe I ever enjoyed this sort of thing. I find myself longing for the quiet of the countryside and quieter songs of praise."

The girl smiled back. "That sounds delightful. I'm Keren, daughter of Beruch of Jericho."

"Mary Magdalene."

"I know." Keren's smile was cheeky. "That's why I came over. I've been hoping to speak with you."

That wasn't always a good thing. In the three days of the wedding feast that had already passed, Magdalene had found herself in any number of conversations with people who were curious about her—either wondering why she'd left the court or why she'd come back. There had been the catty whispers, yes, and the catty not-whispers from the other ladies. Porcia had actually lifted her nose in a sneer and stalked off when Magdalene tried to greet her. Some of the men she'd once known far too well had tried to tell her that country life had made her all the more beautiful, others had said that her new "zealousness" was wretchedly unattractive.

Keren, however, seemed friendly enough, and her gaze was open, devoid of judgment. She leaned closer. "Is it true you travel with Jesus of Nazareth?"

Ah. That was the light Magdalene detected in her eyes. Curiosity not about Magdalene but about the Lord. Her smile came more easily now. "It is. Have you heard Him teach?"

Keren nodded eagerly, that light in her eyes redoubling. "Six months ago. It…it has changed everything. The way I think, the way I view the world."

Magdalene's nod was just as eager. "Yes! He has this way of taking the Law that we all know and showing us what God really meant by it, of showing us how to live with our hearts and not just with our actions."

"My mother and I have been discussing all we learned from Him nearly daily—but we need more instruction, more conversation with other followers. Do you think…?"

Peace eclipsed the anxiety from being in the palace, joy even bubbling up around its edges. Finally, a way to truly do His work here. Magdalene grinned, reaching for her new friend's hand. "I think you and your mother would be very welcome at my villa and with His group of followers if you wanted to travel with us for a while. But over the next three weeks, I will be here with my siblings, and the Lord will be staying at least one of those weeks with us. Please, come. Hear Him, ask Him your questions, dine with us."

"Truly?" Keren bounced on the balls of her feet with excitement, making her seem younger even than she looked.

"Truly. I will be returning there once the wedding week is over, and you and your mother are welcome to come with me."

"I'm so glad I spotted you! I will tell her at once. Actually, will you come with me to meet her? She's on the rooftop, I believe—the din was too much for her, she said. She's been getting horrible headaches ever since my father died last year."

The rooftop? The very thought made a chill sweep her spine, but even so she nodded without hesitation. Talking to this girl's mother about Jesus was more important than the memories the rooftop would bring to mind.

Keeping her smile in place as they climbed the stairs, however, was more difficult than she wanted to admit. She found herself listening for the hiss of demons, the clack of talons—she heard only the cheerful whistle of the wind and a beautiful humming coming from the rooftop haven. The hum gave way to a softly sung psalm of praise as they drew nearer.

"Are you all right, Magdalene?" Keren asked.

Magdalene had paused as they walked by the spot where she had climbed up onto the half wall. She'd been so desperate that day to escape the prison she'd made for herself that she might have obeyed the demons' promptings to jump had she not feared the judgment even more and had she not then seen the soldiers coming with the head of John the Baptizer. How strange to think that in a way, that righteous man's death had saved her life, sent her straight to Jesus. God truly did work in the most marvelous, mysterious ways. She nodded. "The last time I was up here was Herod's birthday, when Salome danced for the king and requested the favor of the Baptizer's head."

Keren's pretty young face twisted. "I have heard of that, though we were not in the area at the time. The princess has spoken of it in my hearing once or twice, with horror."

"I believe she has regretted that request every day since she made it." She had indeed confided in Magdalene just before the wedding that she would be glad to be away from this place and that memory, not to mention out from under her mother's vengeful thumb.

Magdalene had been praying every day that Salome would be a different sort of ruler. A kinder one. She had been praying that her friend would not just feel regret over killing a prophet but would choose to follow his instructions on forgiveness and would herself come to know Jesus.

She didn't know if those prayers would ever lead to her friend's salvation, but she would offer them every day, regardless.

Keren led her onward, toward the lovely singing. They found her mother relaxing on a chaise in the shade of the potted trees positioned up here for that very purpose. She was a woman as lovely as her song, around Imma Mary's age if Magdalene were to guess, and she greeted them with a warm smile that only grew when Keren made the introductions. Her mother's name was Leah, and she took Magdalene's hands in hers as if she were a long-lost friend.

Magdalene reiterated the invitation she'd made to the daughter, and Leah's eyes danced with the same light Keren's had. "Oh, what a blessing that would be! We have so many questions but no one to ask for the answers. But we must know—we must know if following Jesus is worth the sacrifice."

It was, she could assure them of that. Though the question drew her brows together. "The sacrifice?" There always was one, yes—but few realized it at first.

The two exchanged a look, and Leah said, "We have been in betrothal negotiations for the last several weeks. It would be a good match, but he has made it quite clear that if he and Keren marry, she must not seek after Jesus. Certainly never listen to Him again, and not mention Him within their household."

Flames of outrage—both on Jesus's behalf and Keren's—leapt to life inside her. "If he is so threatened by the Truth that my Lord teaches, I would question whether he is really so good a match." Though perhaps that was unfair—perhaps this man had never heard Him for himself, was only listening to rumors.

Keren was nodding though. "It is a big decision to make. On the one hand, he is a good and kind man, and he may simply be concerned that Jesus is a charlatan who would convince me to siphon away household funds to support His ministry. But on the other hand..."

"He could be the Messiah, the Christ," Leah finished, face wistful. "My late husband and I have been watching for Him all our lives, and this man... If He *is* the Messiah, then following Him is worth any sacrifice."

"He is. And it is." Magdalene could make both declarations with ease at this point—for herself. But she spread her hands wide and added, "That is what I believe with my whole heart.

But we each must decide for ourselves what we believe about Him, and whether we can follow Him. You are wise to recognize that."

"The decision has been weighing heavily on us." Keren sat beside her mother and wove their hands together. "But I think if we can hear Him again, we will know what we should do."

"And even until then, you can share what you know with us during the remainder of the wedding feast, perhaps?" Leah asked.

Magdalene's grin was quick and full.

The last time she stood on this roof, she'd nearly been lured into plummeting to her death. But this time, God had given her the chance to speak of everlasting life. Proof, yet again, that He was a God full of life and light.

Though Vaak himself had not ventured to Magdala's market, Magdalene could have mistaken the tall Egyptian manning the spice stall for him, had this version's grin not featured a whole front tooth where Vaak's was chipped. His brother, she soon learned, had been greatly enjoying their town.

Magdalene had insisted to Rhoda that she would do the shopping this morning while Barnabas's wife focused on getting things ready for tonight's feast, and she hummed her way through the crowded marketplace with unbridled joy. Jesus and the Twelve would be spending only one more night with them, so this evening's meal would be worthy of Herod himself. The house would be open for anyone in the neighborhood who wished to come and hear Him. But even beyond that, she rejoiced today because Keren and Leah had professed their faith yesterday and declared that they would rather follow Jesus than bind Keren to a husband who would forbid her from following Him.

The Lord had declared that the angels in heaven were rejoicing at their addition to the kingdom of heaven—and Magdalene was rejoicing here on earth. They would travel with them when the women rejoined the men next month, and she was looking forward to getting know both mother and daughter better. After leaving the spice stall, she paused at one with fresh fruit and lifted a mango to her nose to inhale. The sweet fragrance assured her it was ripe and ready to enjoy.

"I don't know why you're so happy."

Magdalene lowered the mango back to its place and turned with a frown for Judas. She usually enjoyed bumping into one of the Twelve in the towns, knowing they were companions on an important journey. But not Judas. Whenever she ran across him apart from the rest, unease skittered up her spine. And this was why. He never smiled at her, never viewed her as one of the group. Always, always he would imply when Jesus wasn't around to hear that she was a stain on their contingent. "I beg your pardon?"

"About the new women. They're competition, you know. And far better options than *you*."

Competition? She knew her confusion was apparent in her drawn brow. "What are you talking about?"

"You think I don't know why you've stayed so long in our group?" He leaned close—too close—so that his sneer was for her alone. "You think to ingratiate yourself, so that when the Lord comes into His kingdom and reestablishes the throne of David, He'll choose *you* as His first wife. But He won't. This new girl would be a far better choice."

Her brows only fell lower at that. "Where is this idea even coming from? I have no romantic designs on the Lord—and I cannot think *He* has such designs on anyone. He is focused on everyone, not on starting a family."

The look Judas sent her labeled her a dunce. "Now, perhaps. But once He establishes His throne, how will He make it last forever as promised without progeny? But it will not be through *you*."

Heat stung her cheeks, but she wasn't certain if it was over the insult or the assumption. "I would never think— And why are you even thinking such things? The Lord's throne and kingdom are not earthly ones." How could he still think they were? Did he not listen to the Lord?

"Do you not listen to the Lord?" Judas shook his head, taking a step away. "It's right there in the prayer He taught us—'on earth as it is in heaven.' He is preparing the earth to be His kingdom. He will deliver Israel from Rome and perhaps even lead us to such victory that we become the dominant power. He will be even greater than the Maccabees, and we will be His governors. Why else would He be giving us so many lessons on what it requires to be good leaders? To serve, to be humble, to love the people above all."

That wasn't right…was it? That was not how she'd taken any of Jesus's teachings. Yes, there was much talk about the Lord's kingdom, but it was the kingdom of *heaven*. Not earth. He wasn't trying to overthrow Rome like the zealots or other rebels. Was He?

She reached for the mango again, adding it and several others to her basket. Judas was wrong. She knew it down to her core. But he'd never listen to her if she tried to tell him that. "Rest assured that I have no designs on the Lord in that way."

His snort was incredulous. "It doesn't matter if you do. He is too wise to ever stain His lineage with a woman like you."

Her cheeks burned even hotter. Why must he always remind her of her sins? They'd been forgiven. She wasn't that woman any longer. "I would never ask Him to." Which was true. But the proud part of her, the part that craved validation even from this man she didn't like, wanted to point out that nearly every woman named in the lineage of David had a sexual sin against her, from Tamar to Rahab to Ruth—who hadn't actually behaved inappropriately with Boaz, but had anyone seen her there, it would have been assumed. And those assumptions would have gotten her stoned. God often chose the most unlikely of vessels to carry out His plan.

But if she said *that*, Judas would most definitely continue to think her motives for remaining with the group so base. So she bit it back and held her silence, ignoring Judas altogether and paying for the fruit instead.

By the time she turned around again, he had vanished, praise God. She drew in a long breath, wishing she could expel the sour taste he left her with as easily as she did the lung full of air.

Why, why did he always have to come and rob her of her peace? Why did he have to try to dull the brightness of her joy over Keren and Leah?

Well, she wouldn't let him. Not for long, anyway. She resumed her shopping, thinking of the soft light that both women had exuded upon sharing their decisions. Thinking of the good times ahead.

Her spirits had buoyed again by the time she'd filled her basket and left the marketplace, her feet aimed back toward her villa. And perhaps her step would have stayed light and happy, if not for the figure barreling toward her on the road.

Alexander? He was on horseback, galloping her way at such a clip that she stepped off the road altogether, not trusting him not to mow down her and anything else in his way. But he reined in a few feet away, abruptly enough to make the horse toss its head and whinny in protest, and jumped down.

Fury etched new lines in his face as he stormed toward her. "You! Must you ruin *everything*?"

She could only stare at him, agape. She hadn't so much as seen him from a distance since that run-in at the spice stall in Jerusalem eighteen months ago. What of his could she possibly have ruined now?

Her silence clearly did nothing to pacify him. He didn't slow, didn't redirect, and his charge meant he was upon her in another moment. He batted her basket away with such force that it slid off her arm and went flying, scattering fruit and vegetables and spices all over the ground. She might have whinnied a protest of her own, but he grabbed her by the shoulders, wresting her attention from her lost provisions.

His grip was painful for exactly two seconds. Then the realization of it flashed across his face and he let go, stepping back. Still, there was no room for apology in his eyes, not past the anger. "Why? Why did you have to steal her from me too?"

"Who? What have I done?" But even as she asked, a sinking realization settled.

A good match, they'd said. A kind man. But one who would not hear of his bride following Jesus.

"Keren!" he verified with a slash of his hand. "I finally found someone else worthy of marrying. For the first time since you betrayed me, I thought maybe the future held promise. Why couldn't you just leave me that?"

"I…" What was she supposed to say? Her heart ached for all involved—but mostly for him. Why did he have to sabotage his own chance for happiness by refusing to see the Truth of the Lord? Why could he not see that everything he was striving for was useless without Him? Why had he been so prideful that he'd offered sweet Keren such an ultimatum? She shook her head. "I did not know who the man was that she was negotiating with. And I did not tell her what to do, regardless. All I did was provide an opportunity for her to meet Jesus."

A string of curses smote the air, and he spun away from her, raked a hand through his hair, and turned back. "You are at the root of every single disaster that has struck me. I wish I'd never met you. I wish my father had never met your father. Better still, I wish you'd never been born."

She stumbled back a step, the words more a slap than his hand could have delivered. Tears stung her eyes. She knew that he hadn't forgiven her for hurting him, but never had she expected to hear that anyone wished her out of existence entirely.

And still she didn't know how she could answer him. "I'm sorry for anything I've done to cause you injury, physically or emotionally. Please know I wish you only the best. I wish you every happiness."

"Lies! If that were true, you wouldn't have just recruited my chosen bride for that Teacher's harem!"

"Harem?" The heat in her cheeks shifted to pure outrage. "How dare you? Be angry with me all you like—I deserve your ire for the way I behaved at court—but you will *not* impugn the character of my Rabboni! He has never once behaved in anything but the most righteous manner. He is above reproach."

A mask of disgust on his face, Alexander walked backward, toward his horse. "If that were true, He wouldn't have welcomed *you* into His ranks. That is enough to earn reproach."

Magdalene could only curl her fingers into her palms.

Alexander snatched up his reins. "You'll pay for all you've taken from me, Magdalene. One of these days, you'll pay. I may have to bide my time, but eventually I will take from you as much as you have taken from me."

A moment later he was back on his horse and galloping in the direction from which he'd come. She stared after him for a long moment, his threat settling on her shoulders like bricks. Then, weighted down with dark wonder as to what he would do, she bent to salvage what she could of her provisions.

And she prayed, with every bruised mango and split bag of grain that she picked up, that he would focus his anger only on her…and not take it out on those she loved.

CHAPTER FIFTEEN

SABBATH

The world held its breath and sat in silence. That was what it seemed to Magdalene as the dark of Sabbath evening turned into the dim, overcast light of Sabbath day. Elsewhere in the city, people were still enjoying the High Holy Day of the Passover celebration, relaxing together, eating, perhaps even laughing.

Laughing—as if there were any light left in the world.

She hadn't slept, hadn't even tried. She'd just sat at the window in her room at Azur's house, looking out toward Jerusalem. Toward Golgotha. Waiting for something to change, even though it never would.

Hope was gone, dead, buried. *"Mary."* She could still hear His voice in her head, in her heart, but it was only memory. She could see His eyes, sparkling with amusement and insight and that endless, boundless love He seemed to hold for each and every person He encountered…but it was now nothing but her imagination. And there was no way her paltry imagination could do Him justice.

"Mary?"

Dawn was fighting for dominance of the skies, but it was a weak battle. Clouds obscured the sunlight just as they'd obscured the stars all last night. Heavy, ominous, yet dry and empty. It wouldn't rain—rain would be cleansing and life-bringing. No, that was not what Jerusalem deserved now. Only shadow, weight, barrenness.

"Mary?"

When the sun did shine, it would gleam across the white stone of the buildings of the city and seem to dust them with gold, especially at sunrise and sunset. Today, Jerusalem looked instead as though it were coated in ash.

"Mary."

Stranger still, no birds sang, no insects chirped. Magdalene frowned when she realized it. Usually this time of day, even on a cloudy day, there would be a veritable symphony going on in the vineyards. Birds of every feather, singing the praises of the God of hosts. But this morning, there was only a strange hush.

Of course there was a hush. All of creation knew to mourn Him. All of creation held its breath from the pain. Perhaps all of creation wondered if God would destroy them now.

"Sister." Sarah sat beside her, took Magdalene's fingers in her own. "You should eat something. Or perhaps have some chamomile?"

She didn't even bother shaking her head. How could she eat or drink when her Lord was dead? When she would never again sit at table with Him and listen to His teaching?

Her eyes slid closed. If only she had one more chance, one more hour in His presence. She would fall at His feet as she'd done so many times before and wash them again with her tears, kiss them again with all the devotion He deserved. She would ask for one more bit of wisdom. She would ask Him what she was supposed to do without Him. She would…she would…

Her sister smoothed Magdalene's tangled hair back from her face. "At least come out with the rest of us. There will be solace if we mourn together."

She doubted that there could be any solace in anything…but something in her sister's voice finally broke through a bit of the cloud, and Magdalene turned her face from the window.

Sarah knelt beside her, deep shadows under her eyes that said she hadn't slept much if any the night before either. Distress had dug lines into features usually smooth, aging her a decade in the span of a day.

Magdalene's heart squeezed. Here she'd sat all night, isolated and alone in her grief, as if she were the only one feeling this horrible weight of emptiness. How selfish she'd been! Just because she'd met Jesus first, just because He'd banished demons from her soul, did she really think that meant she'd loved Him any more than her sister and brother? They risked everything—their home, their reputation, their very lives— for Jesus too.

Perhaps joining them wouldn't *bring* solace to her soul… but perhaps she could give some. That seemed more like what Jesus would have asked of her, that she step outside of herself, serve instead of expecting to be served. That she love them as He loved them, and allow them to do the same for her because it would grant them that same comfort.

A smile was too much to ask, but Magdalene at least softened her expression and reached out to draw her sister in for an embrace. "Thank you, Sarah," she whispered into her ear. "I will join you in just a few minutes. Let me clean up first."

"May I help? I could brush your hair for you."

Magdalene knew her sister needed to do *something*, to feel useful, to know that she was serving someone else—it was the way she showed her own love. Magdalene nodded, not because her arms were so leaden she doubted her own ability to lift the brush but because she knew it would soothe her sister to be able to perform that basic task. "Please."

They were silent as Magdalene changed into fresh clothes and then sat at her stool, back to her sister. They were silent as Sarah worked the brush through the long tangles of Magdalene's hair. They were silent as they smeared a soothing balm onto the nicks and cuts on Magdalene's palms, from where she'd pounded the earth of Golgotha yesterday afternoon.

"We have guests," Sarah finally whispered as they stood.

Magdalene frowned. "Who? The Twelve?"

Sarah winced. "Eleven, now. John brought word just before dawn—Judas hanged himself yesterday evening."

Magdalene's whole being sagged. She hadn't liked Judas, and he certainly hadn't liked her. They had always been at odds. And he had betrayed their Lord in the worst possible way.

Even so, he had saved her Thursday night. She'd certainly never wished him dead. "I can only imagine the guilt that he felt."

"I know." Sarah squeezed her hand.

Magdalene took a moment to mourn this new loss—the Twelve becoming merely Eleven—and then shook herself. "Did you say John brought the news?"

Her sister nodded. "He and Peter are at his home in Jerusalem with the Lord's mother."

"Did he bring word of her? How is she?"

Sarah's attempt at a smile was more a grimace. "He says she is just…quiet. Not crying, just sitting quietly, praying."

Praying. Perhaps that was the proper word for what Magdalene had done all night, crying silently to God…or perhaps not. She had been demanding answers, but her spirit's ears felt stopped up, deaf to any insight that may have come. Silent, like the day. Like the world without Jesus in it.

"But John is not the only one who has come. Nicodemus, Joseph, and…"

Her brows arched more with each beat. "And?"

Sarah's gaze faltered, fell, her shoulders sagged. "Please don't let it change your decision to join us."

A knot fisted in her stomach. "Sarah."

"Joseph arrived with…with Simon of Cyrene. And…his sons."

"His sons." Magdalene waited for the emotion to swamp her—the anxiety or the fear or the anger. Shouldn't she be feeling one or all of those? The last time she'd faced Alexander, just over a day ago, she had been genuinely afraid. Had Judas not happened by…

This morning, though, those expected emotions wouldn't come. What would he have done? Perhaps something terrible, or perhaps nothing at all. Perhaps the bluster given to him by too much wine would have abated before he could actually harm her, or perhaps he would have taken the revenge he clearly felt he was owed.

Regardless, it mattered nothing now. Everything had changed in that day that stretched long and horrific between then and now. She felt only…bemusement. "Why? Why did they come?"

Sarah spread her hands, palms up, and lifted her shoulders. Knowing Sarah as she did, Magdalene guessed that she hadn't asked why more guests than expected had arrived—she had simply thrown herself into serving them.

Though she might have asked, had she known about that last encounter between Magdalene and Alexander. She might have barred him from the house altogether, or insisted that Azur do so. Those protective, nurturing instincts of hers surely would have reared up, flashed out like lightning, brought color to her cheeks and anger to her lips on her little sister's behalf.

Just as well, then, that there'd been no chance to tell her of that. This was not a day for anger about something as trivial as a drunk accosting her and spewing angry words at her. The King of kings had just been crucified. He lay lifeless in a borrowed tomb. What else mattered?

Nothing.

So then, there was no point in dallying and trying to discern why Simon had brought Alexander and Rufus to their home. She would simply find out. With a nod, she followed Sarah out of her room, along the corridor, and into the main room of the house.

Someone—Sarah or one of the servants—had put out food, but no one had touched it. The plate still sat perfectly arranged on the low table, overflowing with figs and dates and mangos, unleavened bread and dried meats and cheeses. The men scattered about the room looked every bit as carefully arranged, every bit as untouched, as if they were nothing but well-painted and adorned statues.

Until one looked closely. When one did, one would note that Simon still wore the same clothes he'd been in yesterday, when the soldiers had forced him to shoulder the Lord's cross. Dirt caked it where he'd knelt down, sullied its hem. Red-brown streaks stained the shoulder. Blood—the Lord's blood, which had no doubt soaked the cross and then transferred to Simon when he carried it.

Tears blurred her eyes, but she blinked them back and forced her gaze away from his clothing and onto his face. Her breath caught at what she saw there—he looked…haunted. Undone. Desperate. He looked like a man who had encountered his Savior only to lose Him.

Her gaze flew to his sons. Had Simon dragged them here against their will, seeking answers to questions they weren't asking?

No. Rufus sat, hands clasped between his knees, gaze fixed on a spot somewhere before him and brows drawn. She'd never met him before, but she needed no introduction to identify him. He looked so much like Alexander, so much like their father, just a bit older than his brother.

His brother…his brother slouched against the wall, total defeat in his posture. He looked broken, shattered, and it shattered her heart a little more to see him so.

Strange, that. She'd thought her heart already ground to dust by all that happened yesterday. She wouldn't have thought it could fracture any more. And for him?

But all she'd ever wanted, since he first came upon her and Jesus's small early retinue along the road outside Magdala, was for him to listen, to open his heart to the way of salvation. That had never changed, even now. She eased a step away from her sister. "Alexander?"

He startled, straightened, looked her way along with all the others in the room—his family, Azur, Nicodemus, Joseph. Alexander took one step away from the wall but then stopped, his face twisting in distress.

Azur moved to her side. Much as she'd done, he spoke in a whisper—all, it seemed, that the day would allow. "I'm glad you came. Simon and his sons have questions, and while we all followed Him, none of us spent as much time in His presence as you did."

Why didn't John answer them then? But when she looked around, she didn't see the youngest disciple in the room. Perhaps he had left again already. Magdalene dipped her head at the continued attention. Maybe once she'd have taken pride in the months and years spent following the Lord, but she wasn't one of the Twelve, she was no apostle. She'd never been the one entrusted with the authority to heal the sick or cast out demons. What had she ever known but to sit at His feet and listen? "I fear I have little to offer—but what I do have, I will gladly share."

Simon moved forward, so slowly that it seemed he was trudging through mud instead of on overpolished tile. "Please, my lady. I have heard the accusations of the council. My old friend Nicodemus has shared what Jesus told him, about needing to be born of water and the Spirit in order to enter into eternal life."

"Yes, the cleansing of salvation."

Simon waved that away. "All these things I have heard, and they are the words of a prophet, a teacher, a Zealot—if one listens to the accusations of the Sanhedrin. But none of them explain this." He touched his opposite hand to the bloodstains on his shoulder, his face going fierce. "I have suffered for a decade from an injury to my shoulder and upper back. When I knelt to carry this Man's cross, even taking it upon my good shoulder, I feared the usual pain would debilitate me, and the Romans would punish me for my seeming disobedience. Indeed, the old injury screamed with pain for a moment. But then…"

He spun and faced his sons. "You know. You know how I suffered with this."

Rufus and Alexander both nodded, the elder saying to the rest of them, "He has not been able to lift more than a few pounds for years."

"Exactly so. But that man's blood soaked through my garment, and the moment it touched me…" Simon's eyes slid shut, and his face shifted, from question to peace. From doubt to certainty. From darkness to light. "I felt the strength return to my arm, and I stood with that cross on my shoulder as if it weighed no more than a pillow."

He opened his eyes again and turned them on Magdalene, Sarah, and Azur. "How? How could He have healed me while He was collapsed on the ground, too weak to stand? How, when I nearly refused to aid a condemned criminal?"

Azur turned to Magdalene. "This is what confounded me. I know Jesus could heal, but the recipients had to believe, did they not?"

The corners of her lips turned up the smallest fraction. "Did the dead that He raised to life believe while they lay cold and lifeless?" She looked from her brother to the others, each in turn. "I think...I think sometimes it is our faith that makes us well. And sometimes it is seeing the glory of God that ignites that spark of belief. Sometimes He healed for the sake of the one—and sometimes He healed that many would see and marvel and come to faith."

Her gaze settled on Rufus and Alexander. "Perhaps, my lord, you were healed by the sheer power of His blood, despite your doubts, so that your whole family might believe along with you."

"The power of His blood." Rufus stood, shoving agitated fingers through his hair. "I don't understand. Who is this Man, that His blood can do such a thing? A prophet, like Elisha?"

"He is—was... He was more than a prophet." She had to swallow against that past tense, and even speaking it, correcting herself with it, it felt like poison on her tongue. She couldn't bring herself to use it again. "He is the Son of God."

"That was what one of the centurions said yesterday," Alexander muttered, scrubbing a hand over his exhausted face. "I had followed along behind Abba, afraid he would collapse from the effort too, and then we stayed the whole day. After Jesus died, when the earth shook and the heavens darkened, one of the Romans proclaimed Him the Son of God. I didn't even know what he meant, yet now you say the same."

"It means…" She'd thought she'd known, when Jesus was with them, walking on water and calming storms and rewriting everything they thought they knew about the world. What did it mean now, when He lay lifeless in the grave? When the sun didn't even dare to shine nor the birds to sing?

She leaned against her brother's strong arm. "I don't know what it means. This last week, He…He said so many strange things. He spoke of His death, but He kept insisting we would all walk with Him again."

"In the resurrection?" Sarah's fingers laced through Magdalene's. "What else could He have meant?"

"I don't know." Clearly they should have sought out the Twelve for their answers and not relied on her. Her shoulders sagged. "I'm sorry." All their words had been quiet, but these barely even had breath behind them. "I wish I had wisdom to offer instead of confusion."

I wish I had purpose now that He's gone. I wish I knew what any of us could do now.

Alexander shifted a step closer, though then he stopped, as if afraid to close any more of the distance between them. "At the crucifixion yesterday, we all had the strangest sensation. That it was our crimes, our sins that had condemned Him."

Magdalene's brows drew together, and her chin lifted again. "You too?"

He nodded, his larynx bobbing with a swallow. "I thought it just me. But—"

"I felt the same," his father put in. "It was as if, when His eyes moved over me, He called forth my every sin. I could see them, feel them, things I hadn't thought about in years. But then…"

"Then," Rufus picked up, moving to join his father, "it was as if those sins were drawn away from us, like poison from a wound. But put on *Him*."

"How could that be?" Apparently overcoming whatever reticence had held him away, Alexander slid to his family's side as well.

"Like a scapegoat?" Joseph shrugged.

"Or the sacrificial lamb?" Nicodemus sighed and slouched into a chair. "Both, perhaps, rolled up into one. The true spotless Lamb, dying for our sins. To make recompense."

The words settled over the room like a pool of water—salt water that made her eyes burn anew. God had always demanded blood to atone for their sins, sacrifices to remind them of the cost of breaking the covenant with Him. As a child, she had always thought it so cruel that a sweet, innocent lamb would have to give its life for her. For them.

Would God really require this sacrifice? His own Son? It was too heavy a thought to bear standing up. She had to stagger away from her siblings so that she could sink into a seat. She didn't want to believe it, didn't want to entertain the notion that God would really ask such a thing of His perfect Son.

Yet the moment she considered it, so many things Jesus had said snapped into place. Hadn't He spoken of Himself in just this way? And all the times He talked about taking up one's cross and following Him! Had He known? Had He always known this would be His fate?

He couldn't have, not as a mortal man. But of course He did, just as He knew what they were all thinking, knew what awaited each of them. Past, present, future, these had never posed any hindrance to His knowledge.

"Oh, my sweet Jesus," she murmured into the hands she lifted to cover her face. How? How could He ever have smiled, knowing what awaited Him? How could He have spent these years ministering and teaching and offering them all that unbridled love of His, when all along He knew the Father would demand He die for them?

It was a question too heavy for her fragile, weary soul.

CHAPTER SIXTEEN

THURSDAY

They shouldn't have come to Jerusalem for the Feast this year—it was too dangerous. Far too dangerous. They'd all known it, and they'd all tried to talk caution into the Lord, but He wouldn't hear them. He had set His face toward Jerusalem, and nothing could dissuade Him.

Magdalene kept her head down as she maneuvered through the thick crowd of pilgrims, praying with every step that she would go unrecognized. The city had been teeming with opinions since Jesus performed the miracle of resurrection in Bethany a few months ago, and the one thing everyone agreed on was that they should pay attention to anyone associated with the Lord.

The religious leaders paid attention to try to detract from Him and the miracle that the Sadducee high priest wanted more than anything to renounce—because if He could really raise someone four days in the grave, then that lent credence to His claims about an eternal resurrection, in which they did not believe.

He'd made a mockery of them. And now they wanted revenge.

Plenty of others had heard and were curious, wanting to see Him—or one of His followers at least—with their own eyes. A few heard and believed and sought to join their ranks.

The crowds of people that had greeted His entrance into the city on Sunday had been the curious and believing ones… but the longer they were here, the louder the grumbling grew from the Sadducees and even some Pharisees, who accused Jesus of blasphemy. The more violently the crowds around them teemed. The more Magdalene wished Jesus had listened to the advice to stay away from Jerusalem this year.

For safety's sake, the Lord had insisted that He wouldn't take the Feast at the home of any of His known followers, nor would they all eat together as they had in years past. Only He and the Twelve would dine together tonight, in a rented upper room.

It stung, even while she recognized the reasons. He wanted to keep His mother safe above all, and so He insisted they separate while tensions ran so high. Magdalene had been honored when He asked her to take Imma and the other Mary and Susanna to her brother's home for the Feast, to watch over them and keep them company. Joanna and Khuza and little Matthias had journeyed to join them for Passover as well. Which meant there was plenty of joy and laughter to be found at Azur's villa.

The moment she stepped into Jerusalem again, though, it was as though something inside her pulled taut, invisible cords stretched near to breaking. Something was very wrong in the city. Every time she turned a corner, she swore she caught glimpses of shadows that weren't there when she turned her head to investigate more fully. Her imagination?

No. No, she knew those shadows. She recognized them with the same tingling nerves that always warned her minutes before a thunderstorm sizzled overhead.

She pulled her basket closer to her side and tilted her head down a little more, the closer she drew to the Lord's rented room. Sarah and Imma had been cooking nonstop, and they'd sent her with food to add to the Feast for the Lord and His disciples. She knew the Twelve would have purchased many of the items already, but Imma had promised her Son His favorite recipe of unleavened bread and the apple clay He had apparently favored as a child. Having tasted the *charoset* as Imma mixed the chopped apples, almonds, cinnamon, and wine, Magdalene could see why her Rabboni had always loved it. She'd volunteered to bring the basket of food, eager to make certain the men had really seen to everything as they should have.

Now, though, she wondered if she should have let Susanna or Keren bring it—someone less conspicuous. People were definitely looking at her, and she heard more than one whisper that identified her as Magdalene, sister of Azur.

Her family was too well known in Jerusalem, and everyone knew they were Jesus's followers.

Just before she turned the last corner, familiar, angry voices brought her to a halt. She pressed herself to the side of the nearest building, her thudding heart surely audible over the bustling crowds.

"I'm telling you truly, my lord. This supposed Teacher is a hypocrite. He may speak words about purity of heart and mind as well as body, but haven't you seen the women He travels with? They are of the worst reputation." *Alexander.*

A shiver coursed up her spine. She'd managed to avoid him for the past eighteen months, and she'd hoped he had forgotten about her altogether—including his vow for eventual revenge. But still she recognized his voice without any question.

"I am aware of the sins of that harlot called Magdalene." This voice was familiar too, though she may not have recognized it had he not spat the word *harlot* in just that way—he was one of the men who had been dining at Azur's house on that first Passover they spent together. The one who had stormed out when he realized that she was there, and that Jesus would dare to defend her presence.

Her throat went dry. She'd never learned his name, but she'd seen him with the high priest on more than one occasion over the years and knew he sat on the Sanhedrin council.

"She is the worst of them, to be sure." Alexander again. "But I suspect her influence has rubbed off on the other women too. It oughtn't to be borne, my lord. This Teacher is a menace who is leading far too many people astray."

"You think we don't know that? He will be stopped. We need only to gather witnesses."

"I am willing to speak against Him. As to His sinful relationship with that harlot."

Magdalene's breath balled up in her chest. He wouldn't— would he?

A beat, then the other man said, "You saw them engaged in a sinful act?"

"Well…"

"You know the law—they must be caught in the very act, by two or more witnesses."

"I will say I did. And perhaps I can find another witness too."

Heat scalded her neck. Would he really lie before the Sanhedrin? And get someone else to lie with him? Because he had never seen anything untoward between them—he couldn't have, because there had never *been* anything even remotely sinful about her relationship with the Master.

But he was doing exactly what he had threatened—he was seeking to take from her what he knew was most precious. To punish her by punishing those she loved best.

"It may be enough. We have some other witnesses willing to testify to other crimes as well."

What? How, when Jesus had never broken the Law?

Liars, that's what they were gathering. Not witnesses—liars. People who apparently didn't care that they would be breaking one of the Ten Words by bearing false witness against an innocent man. Magdalene waited for their voices to move off, waited another minute to be certain they wouldn't look back and spot her, and then continued around the corner.

She nearly ran into Judas, who was just standing there in the street looking up the alleyway, his brows drawn.

Had he heard Alexander and the councilman too? Was that why he was staring after them? "Judas? Is everything all right?"

Rarely did she speak to him when she didn't have to—but it would be rude to step around him without any acknowledgment.

He turned troubled eyes on her, and his frown only darkened. "I tried to warn Him that you would bring trouble upon His head, but He never listened."

Her fingers tightened on the handle of the basket. "I tried to warn Him too, and offered to leave. Trouble was the last thing I ever wished for the Lord."

"Maybe it's exactly what He needs though. The kick to make Him declare Himself and His kingdom." He took a step away, his eyes contemplative. "Yes…that could be it. His time has come—He keeps saying as much, that His hour is nigh. This is how. They will force His hand, and He will show His true glory. Throw off the bondage of Rome for all of Israel and reclaim the kingdom."

He sidestepped her but not before she saw a new, odd light in his eyes that she would have described as crazed had Judas not always been far too sensible. "That's it. That's what will happen. What *has* to happen…"

He stalked off, still mumbling, leaving Magdalene with yet another source of disquiet. As if Alexander's schemes weren't enough to worry about—what was Judas thinking?

Nothing good, that she knew. All his focus on an earthly kingdom felt horribly wrong. But he would never listen to her about it.

She shook it off and continued toward the rented upper room, taking the outside stairs up to the enclosed area, separate from the host's house below. It seemed most of the Twelve were out about errands or visiting family, because only a few were there, occupied with preparations or study.

Jesus was at the window, however, looking out over the city. She went directly to His side, passing Him the basket. "From Your mother."

He took it with a smile…but a sadder smile than she was used to seeing from Him. "Thank you—and her. I do so long to taste her delicious honeyed bread one more time."

He said it as though He meant "one *last* time." Or maybe she was still too upset by the plotting of Alexander and the council member. "Rabboni—"

"I know, Mary."

He did? Of course He did—He always did. Even so. "Rabboni, I am so sorry. My presence has brought trouble down on You—"

"Your presence, My friend, has never brought anything but joy—to Me, to My precious mother, to all who know you."

She shook her head. "Alexander…"

"He has let his anger lead him down a dangerous path. But it isn't a path you need to worry over. All will be exactly as it must. As it should."

He spoke with the same calm assurance He always did… but it was tinged with sorrow.

She looked around the room, at the table and cushions set up for tonight's Passover. Her heart ached. "I wish we were all together. I wish this cloud did not hover over us." She looked back to His familiar profile. "Rabboni…You know Judas and I have always been at odds, so I don't want this to sound as though I am casting aspersions. But I heard him—"

"I know Judas's intents and ambitions." Another soft, sad smile. "Better even than he does. It brings Me great pain, I admit. But he will do what he wills. He has that freedom. Even so, it will work as My Father has ordained."

She wanted to say something more, to find some way to restore Him to joy, but no such words would come. "Is there anything I can do for You, Lord?"

He turned from the window at that, setting His full attention upon her. "Yes. Stay with Imma as much as you can these next few days. She will need you."

That made her frown even more than what she'd overheard in the street. "You know I am always happy to be with Imma, but—"

"Thank you, Mary. For anointing Me with your tears and your costliest perfume. For providing for My followers and setting such a bright, beautiful example of what it means to follow Me. Thank you for always wanting to be at My feet."

"Where else would I go?" Her words sounded as tearful to her own ears as her vision had grown. "You have the keys to eternal life, Lord. I never want to be anywhere else."

He smiled again, and it had the look of sunshine breaking through clouds. "I know. But you must, for a little while. Go now, My friend. Before twilight falls. Go and celebrate with Imma and your family."

Because He told her to, she would obey. But it took all her love for Him to make her feet move her away, when everything within her screamed that if she left His side now, something horrible would happen before she saw Him again.

Premonition? Prophecy? Empty fear? She prayed it was the last. But the shadows nipped at her heels all the way home.

Was it disobeying the Lord's command to be back in the city after darkness had fallen, given that she was here on His mother's behest? He had told her to stay with Imma—but staying with Imma meant honoring her and obeying her. And she had been every bit as troubled as Magdalene throughout the afternoon and evening, to the point of having to be begged to eat the Feast with them.

The moment the service moved to the meal, she had turned to Magdalene with troubled eyes and whispered, "Something is wrong. Trouble is afoot, I can feel it." She'd splayed a hand over her heart. "Will you go for me, Magdalene? You are faster than I. Just go, peek in at the door, and verify that all is well. Please?"

Perhaps anyone else would have called her an overprotective, fearful mother—but that wasn't ever how Imma behaved, and Magdalene knew she wasn't overreacting.

She had heard the men in the street. She had felt the shadows growing. She had seen the sorrow in Jesus's eyes and heard it in His voice. All was not well. So what would she actually be able to report?

Soon enough, she would know. She was hurrying along the final stretch of street, her eyes already set on the windows aglow in the upper room where the Twelve and their Lord were gathered.

Something shoved into her, hard, knocking her back into the stone of the building at her side, and then pressing her there. "I oughta known you…you'd come here. Be here. Close to *Him*."

The voice made her tense, even as she averted her face from the smell of alcohol on Alexander's breath. "Alexander! You're drunk." She'd never seen him so—though she'd really only known him for a few weeks, three and a half years ago. He could have many habits she didn't know of.

In the light from other gaily lit windows, she could just make out his sneer. He had her pinned against the building, his hands gripping her arms. "All your fault," he slurred. "Father—brother. See what a mess everything is here. Know what a…what a failure. But it's *you*. You took it. You ruined it. This is all your fault! You brought me here, you made me so low! Would that I had never looked on your cursed face!"

"Alexander." She planted her hands against his chest and tried to push him away, slowly enough to keep from angering him any more. "Please."

"I would have forgiven you." He caught her hands, drew them down—pushed them against the building too. "Had you just waited a week. I would have forgiven. We could have married. Been happy. But you had to run off after *Him*."

She opened her mouth to say yet again that she'd run after God, after a life beyond this one, not after a man *as* a man. But she couldn't get a word out before his mouth was on hers, hard and bruising.

He'd kissed her before, once. When he thought they would have a life together, when she'd dreamed of him setting all her wrongs to rights. It had been sweet and heady and fueled the dreams of being his wife.

This didn't even deserve the same name. This wasn't a kiss, it was a punishment. She whimpered, tried to push him away or squirm away or even just break away enough to remind him of who he was.

A good man. A good man who had suffered a series of hard blows, who had let the bitterness eat at him, who had to face his family with that battered pride. A good man who would recall he was a good man as soon as something broke through the haze of wine and pain.

But she couldn't break free, struggle as she might, and he pressed harder instead of easing off, and the darkness—that old, familiar, jeering darkness—was closing in, snapping its teeth at her, laughing in her ears and promising to consume her again as it had before.

No. "*No!*" She managed to scream out that one word before his hand clamped over her mouth. A word for him, for the swarming demons, for anyone else in this godforsaken city who could hear her.

His fingers bit into her arm, and he said something low and threatening that made no sense through the rushing in her ears.

And then he was gone, his weight lifted. She blinked rapidly enough to see that another figure had rammed into him.

She saw a fist lift, land in Alexander's face, and send him sprawling.

A rescuer. God had sent her a rescuer, and she hadn't even had the wherewithal to pray for one. A relieved sob tore through her. She pressed a hand to her mouth to stop it and shifted to better see who had helped her. Jesus?

No. Judas. Of all the people to save her—Judas?

His chest was heaving, and he shook out his hand as if it hurt. He barely glanced her way. "What are you doing here? Go back to your brother's house with Imma Mary."

"She…she asked me to come here."

"He's gone."

"What?" That couldn't be. They shouldn't have been finished with the ceremony already.

Judas was already stepping over Alexander's legs. "For once in your life be reasonable, Magdalene, and do what the Lord instructed! Go home!" He didn't wait to see if she listened, just hurried along, muttering something about, "…give me strength to do this."

Strength to do what? She very nearly followed him, but her task from Imma was far more important. She ran toward the upper room, flew up the stairs, and threw open the door.

Empty. The room was empty, the remains of the meal still laid out on the table, eaten but then abandoned.

No! Where could they have gone? She rushed back down and circled the building, but she saw no sign of any of them.

Hot tears burned her eyes, but she blinked them away. Her arms ached where Alexander had grabbed them, and she could still feel the sting from his beard on her face.

Darkness raced all over the city—she could see it, hear it, smell it. And she had a feeling it would be happy to feast on her if she stood here. Instead, she dashed down a different street than the one Alexander had been on, running as fast as she could out of the city, across the two miles to home.

She could not report to Imma that all was well. But she would at least make sure she reported *something*.

CHAPTER SEVENTEEN

Sabbath

The others continued to muse, to wonder, to talk through all the things they'd heard Him say in soft, hushed tones punctuated by burdensome silences when no one actually had the answers. Magdalene listened with half an ear, but she had nothing to add, not really.

Eventually, she rested her chin in her palms and at least looked at them all again. That was when Alexander, a question on his face and hesitation in his every step, edged her way. His posture made it clear that he would halt, would return to his family's side if she made the slightest indication that he should.

But she didn't. Looking at him now, she didn't see the angry sot from the other night—because he was more than that one mistake, just as she was more than the many she had made before she met her Savior. Jesus had forgiven her, had forgiven them all, up to His dying hour. Who was she to refuse to forgive Alexander for his rough words and actions when he'd had too much wine? Perhaps she would have still been leery had they been alone, but surrounded by their families he certainly posed no threat.

He sat beside her, resting his elbows on his knees. His shoulders bowed forward, and his chin sagged. "I am sorry, Magdalene. So sorry. There are not words enough to express it."

She had known too many men in her life, and most of them would toss those words around to get whatever they wanted, rarely meaning them. They were only ever sorry for the consequences, not for the actions themselves.

Alexander, though, seemed genuinely contrite. More, heartbroken.

"I forgive you."

"You shouldn't. It was unforgivable, what I did to you. I have never in my life felt so…so out of control."

A feeling she had once known all too well. "I understand that. I suffered that very thing for years, Alexander, that was what I couldn't quite explain to you, back…when everything soured between us. I *was* out of control. I'd given myself over to demons, who controlled me like a puppet. But strong drink can be its own demon, can it not?"

He granted that with an inclination of his head. "It is no excuse. I hurt you, and not just that night. I…I must beg your forgiveness for more than that encounter. I must beg it for all of these three years. I have hurt you far more than you realize, and every bit of it on purpose."

Across the room, her sister was urging everyone to get a plate, to eat, to keep up their strength for whatever came next. Everyone refused. Here they were, in the middle of the Feast, and they had declared an unplanned fast. But hadn't Jesus predicted that too? When the Pharisees had chastised His disciples for not fasting, He had said the day would come when the bridegroom was gone, and then they would fast.

He was. And they were.

She blinked it away and turned back to Alexander. "What else then?" She very nearly told him it wouldn't matter, that nothing mattered. That nothing could hurt her now, she was beyond it—the only thing of any import had been taken from her already. But there was power in confession, she knew. Not just the catharsis of it, but the very acknowledgment helped one to put distance between one's sin and oneself.

His head hung lower. "I...when I was in Jerusalem three years ago for Passover—do you remember? I saw you and your sister in the marketplace."

"I remember. We were buying spices."

He nodded. "For a moment, before I recognized you, I just caught a glimpse of you both and was struck by your beauty. For a moment, I thought, 'Ah, all hope is not lost, after all. There are other women as beautiful as Magdalene.' But then it *was* you, and it was like a kick to my stomach. Then when I heard you speaking with such fondness for the Teacher..."

"Oh, Alexander. It wasn't the same sort of fondness. What I felt for Him...it wasn't *feeling* at all, it wasn't the sort of love we experience between siblings or spouses. It was..." She still lacked the words to express it, but she closed her eyes and tried. "He snatched my soul from the very pit of hell. He saved me. And my soul responded with the only thing it could—adoration. Worship."

Words that could label her a blasphemer too, if the wrong ears heard her. God alone was to be adored, God alone worshiped. But Jesus *was* God alone.

She opened her eyes again in time to see Alexander give a slow, thoughtful nod. "I am beginning to understand that now. I didn't then. I was furious. I felt so betrayed. I had given up my whole life in Cyrene, even a potential career in Rome, to come here—for you. To honor the agreement our fathers had made. And when I met you, I thought myself blessed indeed. You seemed to be everything I could have wanted. Everything I needed. In those few short weeks we knew each other, I pinned all my hopes on you."

With effort, she swallowed past the lump in her throat. "Funny—I had done the same with you. Never realizing how unfair it was to expect you, mere man that you are, to be able to fix all the broken places inside me."

He dragged in a long breath. "Perhaps if neither of us had been so foolish…but regardless, it led me to a horrible place. I happened across a few of the religious leaders that day after I saw you in the markets, and they were complaining about the Teacher. About your family, for entertaining Him."

Her throat tightened. "No doubt the very one who had stormed from our home the night before, outraged that my brother would allow a sinner such as I under his roof."

He gave a brief nod. "I am not proud of this, Magdalene, and I beg the forgiveness of you and your family and of Jesus and His disciples too—but I approached them. Offered them what I thought I knew about those sins of yours. All the rumors I'd heard about your group. I offered to bring them whatever other gossip I heard each time I traveled to Jerusalem."

She waited for the pierce of betrayal, the flash of anger at realizing he had done this thing not only the other day, when she overhead him, but all along. Neither came, though clearly he was waiting for it too. She could only let out a long sigh. "You are forgiven."

"How can you say that? Do you not realize what I did? *I* was the one who made certain you were treated so poorly everywhere you went. *I* was the one spreading rumors about your relationship with the Teacher. *I* was the one—"

This time, she did reach over to rest her fingers against his wrist, silencing his quiet but forceful words. "I do realize—and I already knew, at least in part. I overheard you on the street the other day, offering to bear false witness. Do you hear me, Alexander? I knew. And you are forgiven. By me, by my family, by Jesus, by God the Father."

His face crumpled, a muted sob catching in his throat. "You can't. I don't deserve forgiveness."

Her breath may have sounded like laughter on any other day. "No one ever deserves forgiveness. It is grace, a gift, not a payment rendered."

"But—"

"You say you were at Golgotha yesterday, near enough to hear the centurions. Were you near enough, then, to hear Jesus pray for forgiveness for the people killing Him?"

He nodded once.

"And if He is capable of forgiving *that*, do you think anything is beyond Him?"

For a long moment he sat with those words, and Magdalene could almost see him spinning them over and again in his mind, like a coin between his fingers. She waited, giving him time to view it from each angle. To realize that, yes, he might have played a part in her persecution and even in the events that led to that hillside. Yes, he might indeed be guilty of sins deserving of death, as they had all known they were as they watched Jesus take their punishment.

They were all guilty—and He forgave them. The Lord had poured out that forgiveness on them all, just as He had poured out His love and His wisdom these three years.

Now, once again, Alexander had to decide if he would accept it. A gift, even perfectly given, could still be refused or imperfectly accepted. Her fingers still on his wrist, she prayed that this time he would accept. This time, seeing so clearly his guilt, he would also see his need for that forgiveness, and he would take it with open hands.

Maybe that was what it all meant. Maybe that was how the world could go on, if go on it did. Maybe their purpose would have to be in helping people understand that Jesus had offered Himself as a pure, unblemished sacrifice for them.

"Perhaps that's it then."

Had she spoken her thoughts aloud? Her gaze snapped back to Alexander's face from where it had been focused on their hands. His brow was furrowed. "Yesterday—during the earthquake, so the very moment Jesus died—the veil in the Temple was torn in two."

Magdalene sucked in a breath, shocked. "You mean—?"

"Between the Holy Place and the Holy of Holies. The veil meant to divide us from the presence of God. It's gone—everyone was abuzz about it in Jerusalem last night. Some were convinced it was a sign that God has left us, abandoned us forever to Rome."

"No. No, that isn't it." She may have wondered it herself as this silent day crept over the land, but speaking with him had convinced her that couldn't be. Because then Jesus's sacrifice would be for nothing, if God simply gave up on them all and withheld the forgiveness His Son had requested.

Alexander slowly lifted his eyes, until their gazes tangled. A light had reentered his face. "I didn't know what to make of it before. But I think you're right. I think...I think Jesus did exactly what He said He would do. He made a way for us all to reach heaven."

Excitement colored his tone and gave life to his limbs. He sprang to his feet, and her fingers fell back to her side as he hurried toward his father and brother to share his epiphany.

Magdalene nearly smiled as she watched him. She whispered, "Thank You, God," into the space where he'd been. But she didn't get up to follow. Not yet. Perhaps part of her rejoiced that he had finally heard, finally seen, finally accepted.

But the greater part still mourned. No matter how beautiful the sacrifice her Lord had made, it didn't change the fact that it had taken Him from her.

* * *

SUNDAY, BEFORE DAWN

Magdalene looked around her in the lamplight, her eyes moving over each item in the baskets and each woman who would carry them. Most of the oils and spices and aloes waited at the tomb, she knew, but they'd added a few of their own, each bringing something to give. Joanna, Salome, mother of two of the Twelve, the other Mary. She nodded at them at large. "Is that everything?"

Beside her, Sarah wiped her hands on a towel. "It should be. If you've forgotten anything, just send someone back here, and I'll see to it after I've fed the disciples."

Magdalene gave her sister a one-armed hug. "Thank you."

"For what?"

"Seeing to things here while we go to the tomb."

Sarah's lips trembled for a moment, but she pressed them together. "We each have our place, sister. Mine is here, caring for our guests. Yours is where it has always been—at the Lord's feet." She held Magdalene tight. "I go with you in spirit. What you do for Him, you do on behalf of our whole family."

Before she could give in to tears yet again, Magdalene nodded and pulled away, sniffling for good measure. She looked back to her friends. "Ready?"

"Ready," they all whispered.

Joanna lifted the lamp with one hand and rested the other on the soft rounding of her stomach. The other Mary led the way outside, into the predawn darkness.

The odd silence of yesterday had eased. Magdalene heard the soft sounds of insects again, smelled the earth and vines, saw a few pricks of starlight in the western sky, though the eastern horizon was already gray with the coming dawn. Of one accord, they set a brisk pace. Their goal was to get to the tomb at daybreak, so that they'd have the whole day to care for the body of their Lord. If they hurried, they could cover the two miles before the sun crested the hills.

Over the course of the day yesterday, nine of the Twelve had found their way to Azur's home, coming in ones and twos. John and Peter remained in the city with Imma Mary, who could not leave the house while she was unclean from touching her Son's body. From there, they were able to keep an eye and ear alert for any news that may come from the council or Pilate concerning the Lord's body. According to the report that the others had brought with them, the Sanhedrin had convinced the governor to seal the tomb and post a guard to keep them from stealing Him away.

A fact which had caused Magdalene and her friends no little worry. "I still don't know how we're going to get in," Magdalene whispered to Joanna.

Her friend wove their arms together. "Whatever guards they set will simply have to roll the stone away and let us in, won't they? They can't just deny us the opportunity to prepare His body."

"Can't they?" Magdalene shook her head. She would put nothing past them at this point. But she prayed as they walked that it would be as simple as Joanna said.

Silence reigned again as they hurried, but at about the halfway point, Joanna looked her way again. "Are you afraid?"

"Afraid?" To see Jesus, lifeless and still? *Yes.* To face the Roman soldiers who could simply dismiss them if they so chose? *Yes.* To face this unknown future that stretched out before her, purposeless and blank? *Yes.*

"To touch a corpse again. To be unclean. I know after your father…"

Magdalene sucked in a long breath. "I hadn't even considered it." Of course she'd known that preparing the body would make her unclean—the women had all talked about it as they decided who among them would go. They would then simply close themselves together into one portion of the estate or with Imma Mary and keep each other company until they could rejoin the others. But she hadn't thought to make the connection to that other body she had first cradled and then tended. She hadn't heard that horrible accusation sting her mind.

She considered it now, tested her spirit, and found she could shake her head. "I will endure that and more to have this honor. To show Him one more time how much He means to me."

Over and again yesterday she had played it out in her mind, all through that wretched silent day. She hadn't known who else would elect to come with her, but choosing otherwise had never once entered her own mind. She *had* to go. To see Him one last time. To say her goodbyes. Every time she'd closed her eyes, she'd pictured the approach to Joseph's tomb again, imagined how they'd arranged Him inside it in the last light of Preparation Day. She saw Him there on the freshly hewn ledge, wrapped in white linen.

So still. So, so still.

She forced herself to breathe evenly, in and out and in and out, to keep herself from dissolving into tears again even now. But no—she'd fought them off all day yesterday, she wouldn't succumb now, when she needed to be able to see clearly to avoid stumbling in the dark.

Over and again, she'd imagined going through the anointing process with the other women. They would be slow and meticulous, careful to bathe every inch of Him in the precious oils and aloes and spices that would preserve His body as long as possible. Perhaps even to the end of time—because how long would that be?

He had said that some of them wouldn't taste death before they saw the kingdom of God, didn't He? The end would come soon then. God would declare the final Judgment, and no doubt His Son would return then in victory to reign over them all. Would He call up this abused body that they would tend, or would He have a new, heavenly one?

They bypassed the city and climbed toward the tomb, Magdalene's tired muscles aching with the effort. She hadn't slept again last night, though she had tried. She couldn't. Every time she closed her eyes, she saw His agony. She saw His death. She saw Him laid out on that rocky ledge in the tomb, and she'd wanted to weep.

Maybe…maybe she would just stay there. Wait for that End of Days, wait for that Judgment to come. She would curl herself up at the Lord's feet and wait for Him to come and reclaim His body. That way she'd be the first to see Him.

Longing made her muscles that much heavier. All she wanted was to see Him. Just one more time. She didn't know what she'd say, though she had come up with a thousand different options during the long hours of the night. Useless, all of them. She would simply fall at His feet and anoint them again with her tears, that was all. Cling to Him.

Dawn kissed the horizon, making the sky blush. She watched the sun stretch its golden wings as they climbed the final part of the path, then she looked over to the rock-hewn tomb.

She came to a halt along with her friends. They had expected a large stone rolled over the mouth of the opening, soldiers at alert on either side.

What she saw instead were two Roman soldiers unmoving on the ground, eyes open, chests rising and falling, but otherwise moving not at all.

And the tomb—the tomb was open, the rock rolled to one side.

Magdalene stumbled forward ahead of the others, her heart pounding in her ears. What had happened? Something—*something* had happened, but she didn't know what. She peeked into the tomb, but the golden arrow of sunlight told her all she needed to know.

She spun, eyes wide, heart pounding for escape from her chest. "He's gone! Someone has—someone has stolen Him away!"

CHAPTER EIGHTEEN

Her friends looked every bit as distressed as she felt. Joanna dropped her lamp, the other women their baskets.

The other Mary grabbed Magdalene's arm, her face urgent. "Quick, Magdalene. You run to Jerusalem to tell Peter and John. We'll tell the others at your family's home. Someone will know what to do."

"Yes. Yes, I…I will." She didn't pause for further instruction, just took off running back down the path, not slowing even when she heard her friends cry out in surprise as she reached the bottom of the hill. Likely one of the guards had stirred, but they wouldn't attack a knot of unarmed women. If anything, perhaps they could offer an excuse as to how, *how* they'd let this happen!

She flew along the road into the city, unaware of the effort it must have taken to move her tired muscles, to drag breath into her lungs. None of that mattered. All she could feel was the pounding of her heart, crying out with every footfall, *No, no, no!*

Was it not enough that they had killed Him? That they had punished Him for her sins, for all their sins? Was it not enough that they'd pierced His side and put a crown of thorns upon His head? Was it not enough that they'd made them leave Him in His tomb without the proper preparation because of the Sabbath? Must they now rob her of this final chance to pay Him her respects?

Before she was quite aware of what was happening, she was pounding on the door to John's house. He opened it on her third knock, and only took one look at her before calling over his shoulder, "Peter! It's Magdalene!"

"They've taken Him." She lifted a hand, meaning to clutch his arm, but she was shaking too badly even to grab hold of him. "They've taken His body, and we don't know where!"

"What?" Peter pushed into the doorway, out of it. "No! Take us! Take us at once!"

She glanced past them, toward the interior of the house. "Imma?"

"She'll be all right. She is praying." John slipped out too, closing the door behind them. "Quickly, Magdalene, show us the way."

She nodded and pivoted to take the lead, running again even though she had no idea where the energy to do so was coming from. None of them tried to talk as they made the short journey back to the tomb, and as they neared it and she pointed ahead, the men both passed her by.

She staggered to a halt in the garden several yards away, leaning against another rock outcropping, eyes pinned to the opening.

She had hoped that, somehow, it would be different when she arrived here with John and Peter. But the stone was still rolled away, the guards still immobile on the ground, and now the other women were gone, no doubt on their way back to the villa. John reached the tomb first and bent down to look inside but didn't enter. Instead, he turned to wait for Peter.

He was only a few steps behind, and he didn't hesitate—that was Peter, always bold, always the leader. If anyone knew what to do, it would be he. He ducked inside, vanishing into the opening. John followed close on his heels.

A wave crashed over her—exhaustion, despair, sorrow, all pounding into her at once, bowing her under their weight. The tears she'd been holding back came surging up, blurring her eyes and curving her spine.

Distantly, she heard Peter and John exiting the tomb again. Peter, saying something about "…what it means." John, sounding so young and hopeful, asking, "Do you think…?"

Magdalene had no room between her tears for wondering what they meant or thought, certainly not for youth or hope. She felt ancient, hopeless, ready to crumble into dust as she waved them away when they paused before her. Let them return to their houses or to hers or…whatever else they wanted to do. She couldn't walk another step. Not unless it was a step that would lead her to Jesus.

Where was He? What had they done with His body—and who? Who would steal it away?

Peter and John's footsteps faded to nothing, leaving Magdalene alone again but for the two stunned guards. Thinking of them made a shiver course through her. Perhaps they had answers. Perhaps, when they regained their senses, they would be able to tell everyone what happened.

She'd barely glanced into the tomb before. Now she turned that way again, gripping the edge of the opening with a weary hand. Though she could barely see through her tears, she noted something strange—the Lord's burial clothes. They were still there, folded neatly on the shelf of rock. The linen with which He'd been bound, even the square of cloth they'd laid over His face.

Why would those have been left behind?

She blinked to try to make sense of it, but her confusion only grew. Now, in addition to the white cloth, she could have sworn she saw two men clothed in a white so bright and new it seemed to shine, one where the Lord's head had been, one where His feet had been.

Was she hallucinating? She shook her head, but the vision didn't clear from before her eyes.

"My lady," one of the men said.

"Why are you weeping?" the other asked.

Their voices…their voices sounded like rushing wind. She didn't just hear them with her ears but felt them on her skin, tasted them on her tongue, caught a whiff of them in her nostrils. Magdalene stumbled back a step. "They…they have taken away my Lord, and I don't know where they've laid Him."

Her skin prickled the more she tried to look at them, her already ragged breath catching and heaving. She spun back around, away from the tomb and toward the garden path, trembling too much to face them for another moment.

A figure blocked her way, indistinct in the soft morning light and through the veil of her tears. It wasn't one of the guards, back on his feet, that she knew. This figure wasn't clothed in the short tunic of a fighting man, but in a long one. A gardener? She tried to wipe some of the tears from her eyes to clear them, but it was no use. More raced to take the place of the ones she wiped away.

"My lady," the newcomer said, "why are you weeping? Whom are you seeking?"

The man's voice somehow undid her still more, making the tears come faster, harder. "Sir, if you have carried Him away, tell me—please, I beg you! Just tell me where you have laid Him and I...I will take Him away, I will tend Him, I will..."

What? What did she really think she could do on her own? Lift His body and return it to this grave? She could barely lift her own head at this point. She turned from him, knowing that even if he could give her that information, it would be useless to her.

The man came a step closer, and the sun brightened. He lifted a hand, and the wind whipped around her, making her blink against it, drying her tears. Goose bumps rose on her arms, her legs, the back of her neck.

Those men in the tomb...who were they? And this man who stood before her now...was he really the gardener?

"Mary."

Her eyes cleared. Her soul cleared. Her exhaustion cleared. She spun back to face Him, and laughter exploded from her lips. "Rabboni!" It was *Him*! Jesus! She threw herself forward, joy so overwhelming that it pushed her straight downward, at His feet.

She reached to wrap her hands around His ankles, that laughter now taking the place of her tears. Because she knew— even though it defied all logic, all reason, all rules of nature, she knew it was Him. The voice, yes. But His feet—how many times had she sat at His feet? She'd bathed them with her tears, she'd dried them with her hair, she'd kissed them and anointed them.

Now they were not only the feet at which she'd worshiped, but she could see too the place where the nail had pierced them, and those wounds nearly brought the tears surging through the joy again. Her precious Jesus, her Lord and Savior.

But He was here—raised, living, resurrected!

Before her hands could touch Him, He backed away, laughter of His own in His throat. "Don't cling to Me, Mary. I haven't yet ascended to My Father."

She tilted her face up, her hands still yearning for one touch. "Lord?"

He smiled down at her, reached out His own hand, and touched a single fingertip to the center of her forehead.

Light cascaded through her soul. It was like a million suns all rising at once, all the waters in the world bubbling together and baptizing her, all hope and love and peace joined together in a single song that exploded through her whole being. She sat back on her heels, just looking at Him.

He was clothed in white as brilliant as what the men— angels?—in the tomb had been wearing, but it was *Him*. The same Lord she knew so well. The same face she'd watched through the years. The same voice that had said her name countless times.

The Son of God. The Light of the World. The Word made flesh, which would echo forever through her soul. The King of kings and Lord of lords.

He had died for her sins, she'd known that already. He'd paid the price, taken the punishment.

But it hadn't defeated Him. Somehow, He had defeated death. His kingdom, that kingdom of heaven that He'd always spoken of…He'd just brought it to them. No wonder He had said that some of them wouldn't taste death until they saw it—here it was, standing in this garden with her, outside the tomb, that empty, empty tomb.

Jesus's lips curved up into the most beautiful smile she'd ever seen. "You have your purpose now, My friend. Go, tell My disciples that you have seen Me."

The thrill of it brought her to her feet. "Truly, Lord? You would entrust me with this message?"

His chuckle eclipsed the birdsong in sweetness. "I can think of no messenger more deserving. You were always the first to worship at My feet—now you will be the first to proclaim the Good News. Tell them I will see them in Galilee, before I ascend to My Father and their Father, to My God and their God. Will you do that for Me, Mary?"

Would she? She had to press her joined hands to her mouth to keep her laughter from rendering her incomprehensible, that spot on her forehead where He'd touched her still tingling, a fount of new joy every second. "You know I will, Lord.

I will proclaim it to them and to all who will listen for all my days."

"I do know. You will shout it far and wide, and your love for Me will make you known to generations."

She shook her head, letting her hands slip down, knowing her smile likely split her face. "It doesn't matter if anyone ever knows my name, Lord—so long as they know Yours."

"And that is why you get this honor. Go, My friend. Go and share the Good News."

Part of her wanted to linger—how could she leave as long as He was there? But the greater part thrilled, new energy bursting through her. She knew He wouldn't stand long in this spot anyway, and she had no desire to watch Him leave.

No. All her desire was to obey that precious, amazing command He'd just given her. She flew down the path, back to the disciples, to her family, to her friends. She didn't bother trying to plan out how she would tell them.

The truth would speak for itself, and there were only two simple words necessary to contain it. "He lives!"

Two simple words that would light the rest of her life.

Letter from
THE AUTHOR

Dear Reader,

When I sat down to learn what I could about this mysterious woman in Scripture, I was pretty shocked to open my first research book and learn that many people throughout history have believed that Mary Magdalene is not only equated with the woman who anointed Jesus's feet with her tears and dried them with her hair, but she was also one and the same as Mary of Bethany, sister of Martha and Lazarus. For the purposes of this series, I couldn't explore that theory, but it was widely embraced all the way up until the 1800s!

I found the reasoning and explanations thought-provoking, and did my best to preserve some of the insights gained through that reading in this book, while also never stating that they're the same. I chose names for her siblings that are variations of Martha (which means "lady" in Hebrew; I chose "Sarah," which means "princess") and Lazarus (Azur and Lazarus are variations of the same name), and I positioned their estate outside Jerusalem, where Bethany is located.

Whether or not this theory is the truth, there is a lesson I know we all need to dwell on, and which has inspired me in ways I can't explain. As we go through our lives, through our jobs, as we move throughout our families, are we making sure that first and foremost, we're worshiping at His feet, like Mary Magdalene? Are we always there, eager to soak up His wisdom and hear His teaching? Do we give Him all our adoration and worship, all honor and praise for what He did for us?

What we know for sure about Mary Magdalene is that Jesus cast seven demons out of her, though even that could be metaphorical; "seven" is often used in biblical language to mean "all" or "complete," so it could simply mean that He cast out all the evil forces from her. Regardless, I found myself intrigued by the idea that these demons may have either been or manifested themselves as what we today would call psychological disorders. I chose to preserve the idea of literal demons, but I also drew on the seven most common disorders to showcase how they might have appeared: anxiety, depression, dissociation, eating disorder, paranoia, PTSD, and OCD. These obviously weren't named in the text, but you'll find them appearing in everything from her blacking out to her tracing the henna designs on her arm obsessively when she is feeling unclean.

The other truly remarkable thing about this woman is that though the four Gospel writers tell the story of the empty tomb from very different perspectives, one detail they all mention is that Mary Magdalene was there. The other women are only occasionally named, but the Gospels are all quite clear that she was there, she saw the angels, and she was the first of the group of followers to see the risen Lord. She was the one given the charge to carry the news of His resurrection to the others.

Why, I found myself wondering, was she entrusted with this sacred, mysterious, joyful message? Why her above all the rest? That was where that reading of the full Mary really helped me to understand why she would be given this honor: because that Mary, who was always to be found at the feet of Christ, had proven herself so full of selfless love, so full of adoration, that she was the natural choice. She never clamored for position or was stained by ambition. She never got distracted by anything else. Her sole purpose, after she encountered Christ, was to follow Him. And so, she became the means by which that best of Good News reached first the disciples and, through them, the world.

Throughout history, Mary Magdalene has become known as the "Apostle to the Apostles," because she brought the Gospel to them that beautiful Sunday morning. I love that and wanted to capture a bit of the joy of it in these pages.

You'll also note that I chose to weave her life closely to Joanna and the court of Herod; this is because Magdala was in fact the town nearest to Herod's court, and it would have been peopled with high-ranking courtiers. For Mary to be known by the name of the town implies that she was a woman of means from the town, perhaps even the wealthiest woman from the region.

I drew some other connections that may or may not be fact; Simon of Cyrene is mentioned in three of the Gospels in the crucifixion narrative, but traditions disagree on whether he went on to be a believer. Some think he didn't, while others insist that since he is the father of Alexander and Rufus from Cyrene—early missionaries mentioned in the Epistles—he must have come to believe. I decided to run with that more connected story, and to plant Alexander in my novel as someone who had his own redemption story that would eventually send him and his brother out into the world for Christ.

I hope you've enjoyed my interpretation of Magdalene's story…and most of all, I hope it's reminded you, as it has me, of where we should always seek to be: at His feet.

Cheers,

Roseanna M. White

A SCHOLAR'S VIEW OF HEROD

The long shadow of Herod the Great fell across the entire first century. Speaking of this period without recognizing Herod is impossible. But he was not considered "great" because the people loved him or thought him to be a fair and gracious ruler. Far from it. Herod's moniker and legacy came only from Herod's passion for building.

Herod was born in 72 BC, the son of a Jewish mother and an Edomite father. While raised as a Jew, his ethnic background on both sides of the family was Arab. Because Herod's father had a good relationship with a Roman general and dictator, Julius Caesar, he was appointed governor of Galilee. What Rome wanted, Herod provided, including taxing the people. When he became entangled with the Hasmonean Jewish ruler John Hyrcanus II, Hyrcanus wanted to put him on trial for murder. Herod barely wiggled out of the possible disaster. Even though enjoying the backing of Rome, he was condemned by the Sanhedrin for brutality.

The most notorious deed during Herod's reign was the slaughter of innocent children in Bethlehem. Fearing that a possible messiah had been born there, Herod dispatched soldiers to kill all newborn males.

Despite his cruelty, Herod the Great's accomplishments were important. His works were built both inside and outside of Israel, but his most noteworthy creation was expanding and rebuilding the Second Temple in Jerusalem. Jesus's disciples were so impressed that they exclaimed, "Teacher, see what manner of stones and buildings are here!" Jesus answered, "Do you see these buildings? Not one stone shall be left upon another, that shall not be torn down." (Mark 13:1-2) Forty years later the Romans did exactly what Jesus foretold.

Herod built seven palace complexes, three of which I have visited. Perhaps the most famous is the remnant of Masada that overlooks the Dead Sea. Somewhere around 22 AD, Herod also began developing Caesarea on the Mediterranean coast. A special box seat with the name Pontius Pilate was found in the amphitheater built there. I walked through the remains of what once had been Herod's palace a short distance from the theater. A Roman circus or racetrack stands on the other side. I quickly recognized that Herod's palace was located next to the sea on purpose, built to prevent an attack on his life. Herod knew what he was doing!

Herod's most beloved palace stood high on the top of a giant mound, which looks like a giant volcano, and was named after him. Herodium remains one of the major local tourist sights to this day. In Herod's time, the grounds featured a Roman bathhouse and were covered with lush greenery. Standing on the top of the hill, I could see for miles.

It must be acknowledged that Herod did a number of important things for the populace that can be measured against his harsh cruelties. During a time of famine, he ensured that food was distributed evenly from the royal supplies. He cut taxes twice and established a period of prosperity.

When Herod began experiencing various excruciatingly painful symptoms and his health deteriorated, he was taken across the Jordan River to Callirrhoe where he was bathed in a vessel filled with oil. Even though he was thought to be dying, Herod recovered, crossed back over the Jordan and returned home—only to die later. Scholars disagree on the date of his death, but it was at most a handful of years after the birth of Jesus.

The funeral procession for Herod was sumptuous and must have been something to behold. His body was placed on a golden bier decorated with sparkling stones of every variety for transport. Behind the escorts marched the entire army as if going to war. Bringing up the rear were servants carrying baskets of spices. The long procession climbed the steep slopes of Herodium to bury him at the top, where soldiers in full battle dress guarded the crypt.

We can only make an assumption, but if Herod's funeral followed Jewish customs, he was not embalmed, and the body was left in its natural state after being cleansed. A tallit—prayer shawl—would have been wrapped around him before he was placed into a wooden casket of some sort. Jews believed, then and now, that "from the earth we came and to the earth we return."

Scholars have suggested that, during his life, Herod was motivated by a vision of raising the Jewish nation to a new height as part of the emerging new Roman world order. On one hand he portrayed himself as a "Jew of the Jews," while on the other hand, he placated Rome and complied with Roman customs. Herod pressured the Jews to accept Greek sports and games as well as paying homage to statues and temples dedicated to the Roman emperor. Herod tried to keep a foot in both worlds, failing to appreciate Jewish resistance to anything that smacked of idolatry.

Herod the Great was succeeded by his son Herod Antipas, who would have reigned during the time of Mary Magdalene. Like his father, Antipas was a builder, but garnered little or no affection from the Jews that he governed. He founded and built the city of Tiberias that stands to this day. Unfortunately, he built it on top of a Jewish cemetery, only exacerbating hostility from the Jews. They shunned this city named after Emperor Tiberius as an unclean place.

Called simply Herod, and not Antipas, in the New Testament, he put John the Baptist to death. Of course, the conflict with John and his subsequent demise only brought more tension to the land. The average citizen had no recourse to oppose the imposed rule of the Herods unless they wanted to die. The Romans had already conquered Israel and stood firmly behind the rulers they imposed. All of this came to a head in 68 AD when a nationwide uprising fought the Romans. Of course, the war ended two years later with the complete destruction of Jerusalem. While the New Testament only hints at this event, Mary Magdalene, the Apostles, and the first Christians lived through these times of extreme turbulence.

Yet, thanks to their perseverance, Christianity survived and grew into the great faith we know today.

Fiction Author

ROSEANNA M. WHITE

Roseanna M. White is a bestselling, Christy Award-winning author who has long claimed that words are the air she breathes. When not writing fiction, she's homeschooling her two kids, editing, designing book covers, and pretending her house will clean itself. Roseanna is the author of several mysteries and a slew of historical novels that span several continents and thousands of years. Spies and war and mayhem always seem to find their way into her books…to offset her real life, which is blessedly ordinary.

Nonfiction Author

ROBERT L. WISE, Ph.D.

The Rev. Robert L. Wise, Ph.D., is the author of thirty-five books and numerous articles published in English, Spanish, Dutch, Chinese, Japanese, and German. On the internet he weekly publishes *Miracles Never Cease* and monthly presents live interviews on YouTube with people who have experienced divine interventions.

TENDER MERCIES: ELIZABETH'S STORY

BY TEXIE SUSAN GREGORY

Elizabeth raced into the courtyard. Whirling around a corner, she nearly knocked a small woman to the ground. She reached to steady her as they teetered. "Oh, Imma, I'm so sorry."

Imma regained her balance, pulled her into a hug, then gently pushed her away and frowned. "You've been outside. Have you finished your morning duties?"

Elizabeth winced. "I was—"

"And we've told you repeatedly to walk, yet you nearly toppled me over."

"But—"

"I'd never guess you're turning fifteen today."

The playful glint in Imma's eyes and the corner of her mouth inching up gave her away.

"I thought I was really in trouble and that you'd forgotten my birthday."

"Abba is not the only one who can play. Besides, I'll never forget all the work I did fifteen years ago to bring you into the world. Someday, you'll know your own child pains and understand."

Elizabeth gave her a quick kiss, then spun in a circle. "Maybe. But I'm not even betrothed yet." She grinned, snatched a fig, and bit into it. "And today, I'm eating only figs and pomegranates." Sticky juice smeared her chin.

Imma's silence surprised her. "Is all well, Imma? You're so serious."

"Elizabeth, dear one, your abba has decided that today is—"

"Have you told her?" Abba stood in the doorway, his feet apart—a soldier's stance despite his priesthood. His voice was gruff, its heaviness further dimming the morning's joy. Where was Abba's usual smile? Had Imma's illness returned?

Elizabeth shivered. Icy chills like winter rain slid between her shoulders and down her spine. The last time she'd known this shiver was when Imma almost died of a wasting sickness.

"You tell her." Imma's eyes flashed at him with rare anger. "You chose. You did this."

Elizabeth's fingers tightened around the fig. Pulp oozed through her fingers. "Tell me what? Chose what?"

"Bethy." He tilted his bearded chin down and locked his green-eyed gaze on her. "Today is not only your birthday. It's also your betrothal day. We rejoice with you!"

She choked on a laugh. "Dearest Abba, I haven't chosen anyone."

A seldom seen frown appeared on his face. "It is not for you to choose." He pointed to his chest. "I am the abba. I decide what is best for you."

Imma bustled to her side. "He will be here soon. Come, let's prepare you to be a lovely bride."

A lovely *bride?* Her laughter fled as her eyes narrowed and her insides knotted. "He who, Imma? Do I know him?"

Abba cleared his throat. "He's a priest. It's fitting for the daughter of a priest marry a priest since we are descendants of Aaron, and you carry the same name as Aaron's wife. Remember, too, your imma is of the line of David. You must marry a man equal in worth to you."

Those were familiar words, but the others—*groom…bride… marry*—were for next year or the next. Heart racing, she began to tremble. Surely it was not Zechariah, the only unmarried priest she knew. "But do I know him? Does he live here?"

"We know you want children. He's never married and wants a young wife able to give him many heirs. He's respected in our community, teaches at the synagogue, quite a scholar—spent the last five years studying with the great rabbi Hillel. He bought the empty house near his father so he could study in peace. You'll have your own home, no demanding mother-in-law to please. I knew you'd like that." His laugh was forced.

The only person she could think of seemed ancient. It could not be him. She clutched the table in front of her, felt blood drain from her face and her hands turn clammy cold. "No, I—"

Abba held up his hand warning her not to speak. "It is done. We have agreed on terms, and I have the gold ring he gifted you. Accept it as the obedient daughter you can be." He removed the slender band from the sash around his waist.

A ring—symbol of bondage. Servitude. Subjection.

Iron determination lined his smile. She knew this smile. Rare. Implacable. Abba was law or laughter. Nothing in between. Once he decided, neither tears nor pleading changed his mind.

"Yes, you know him and his family. He joined us last Shabbat."

She sorted backward for the blurred memory of last Shabbat. Then she remembered. He was short, with thin hair, delicate as a gazelle.

Zechariah.

His sister, Myrah, her dearest friend—a beauty, always laughing, often mischievous. Her older brother? Unremarkable. Invisible. Nondescript. If Myrah spoke of him it was to boast of his diligence in studying in Jerusalem or when home, at the synagogue. He had nodded to her on the rare occasion their paths crossed but never spoken.

"He's boring." If Myrah knew of this and had not told her, she'd never forgive her. "And ancient!"

"He's only a few years older than you—seven, I think—a suitable age, a fine match. He is a good man." Abba's eyes warmed with tenderness. "I'm trusting him with my greatest joy, Bethy. You.

"I have accepted his *mohar*. His gift for the privilege of marrying you was of the finest craftsmanship." The warmth vanished. "It is settled." He crossed his arms, stone-faced. A sharp nod punctuated his words.

All hope of wheedling him to her way fled. Dazed, she allowed Imma to guide her into the house. A new tunic—shroud of her girlhood—was slipped over her head. Her hair was brushed, rose-scented oil rubbed into her hands.

She roused to the inescapable reality as silver bracelets—chains—were secured around her arms and wrists, binding her to a life she did not want, forcing her acquiescence, hurting her pride. She—the acknowledged beauty of the town, educated above the others, only child of indulgent parents—given to a man who looked twice her age.

Elizabeth clutched Imma's hands, holding them to her heart. The silver bracelets jangled as they slid down to her elbows. "Imma, please stop Abba. Why is he doing this to me? I don't want to marry that old priest. Can't you say something? Convince him this is wrong? I will be miserable forever. Please, Imma?"

Imma drew her close, nestled her against the soft shoulder. "If I'd been aware of his plans in time…" She sighed. "Now it is done, and, child, he's only a bit older than you. It seems hard but Adonai will bring good from it. I promise you this. Perhaps you will be the one to bear the true messiah."

"But it's happening so fast."

"Zechariah's abba has been ill and wants to see his children settled in case he does not recover."

"But—"

"Elizabeth, you are becoming a strong woman, stronger than you yet know. Accept that it is done. We will make the best of this—a trip to Jerusalem for the finest cloth and sandals—your abba will not complain. We will even purchase household goods and linens. Your Nazareth cousins, Nathan and Tavi, will attend the wedding next year. I'm sure they'll bring their daughter. Would you like Anna to be one of your attendants?

Isn't she eleven? A little young to be a bridesmaid but she's certainly still a virgin."

This must be how a rabbit felt beneath a hawk's wings. Nowhere to hide, no escape, no defense, only the darkening shadow, wings thrumming death as it circled, lowered, talons outstretched to snatch an innocent's life.

If she was as strong as Imma said, she'd refuse to agree to this marriage. If Adonai wanted good from this, He'd stop it now.

Make the best of it? New clothes and fire tongs mattered little.

She wrapped her arms around her middle, and sobbing, doubled over. Abba had always doted on her even if she was a girl. Had she angered him that he would do this?

Spent, she calmed as Imma pressed a cool cloth to the back of her neck, washed her face and dried her eyes. A growing discomfort warned that the day would worsen.

"Imma, my cycle will start soon." She grimaced as a cramp clutched her belly.

"Sit. I will bring you a tea of chamomile to ease your cramps."

"Abba?"

"The men will have to wait. You cannot faint during the ceremony, but we need to hurry before you are unclean."

She waited until she was alone and stood. Would jumping and twisting cause the blood to flow sooner? She sat. It would only postpone the inevitable.

Too soon she joined her unwanted groom and their parents before a few neighbors.

Zechariah fidgeted, as nervous as she was reluctant. Maybe he did not want this either. Hope rose. Fell. His voice sounded strong and sure as he recited Hosea's words inviting Elohim into their covenant.

"I will betroth you to me forever; I will betroth you in righteousness and justice, in love and compassion. I will betroth you in faithfulness, and you will acknowledge the Lord."

Forever sounded…endless. Elizabeth swallowed the bile rising in her throat.

Too soon wine was poured in Abba's favorite goblet and placed before the groom's father, who handed it to his son. Too soon Zechariah wrapped both his thin hands around the goblet's bowl and held it out in front of her.

Her stomach cramped. She did not want the cup. She did not want him. She did not want to be here. She wanted to curl up under a blanket with a warmed sheepskin. She clamped her jaws together until they ached—imprisoning her sobs.

"This cup I offer to you." Uncertainty tinged his voice. He must have guessed that she did not want this.

She stared at his offering, her girlish dreams fading. Accepting the drink, she'd place her life and those of her children in his delicate hands. Rejecting it, she insulted everyone.

By Hebrew law, the choice was hers. And hers as well, the choice to displease and humiliate the two people she loved most, the two she never doubted loved her. Refusing this groom exacted a price she'd not pay. Her beloved abba would be dishonored. Zechariah too would be shamed, and Myrah, furious on behalf of her brother, would no longer be her friend.

She allowed him to press the goblet in to her trembling hands with his icy fingers. Hypnotized by the rippling redness inside the cup, she hesitated. If she drank, her life was over, consigned to this man she did not know, who did not know her.

Abba's words rang in her mind. *"I'm trusting him with my greatest joy. You."* Abba's love was a treasure more precious than Hebrew law.

She sipped from the cup.

Her husband's warm, full voice intoned the traditional words. "You are set apart for me according to the law of Moses and Israel." Joy and relief, evident in his tone.

Now betrothed, she fumbled with the required veil that covered her hair, wishing she could pull it all the way over her face. Did the others realize she did not want this? Could they read resignation in her face? Were her eyes red, her face grief-pale?

Among the well-wishers, she added her name to the *ketubah*. She watched the ink darken as it dried. The signed contract could not be broken. She was betrothed, a bond inescapable as marriage.

Abba cleared his throat—a sure tell that what followed would be unwelcome. This time he did not meet her eyes. Suspicious, she tensed. What could be worse than the commitment she'd made? She looked toward Imma, who watched with alarm.

"Zechariah has already fulfilled the ketubah contract. The house is prepared, and his abba and I have agreed the wedding will be within six weeks—"

Imma's gasp might have been heard in the next town. "*Six weeks? Not a year?*" She grasped her head as if in agony. "For my daughter's wedding? It's unheard of! How can I—"

Abba silenced her with a single sideways glance and continued.

"…as soon as his sister, Myrah, returns home. Daughter, your husband wishes to marry immediately."

"Your husband wishes.…" What of my wishes? I do not wish to be married or spend my life with this old man or leave my imma's house. She bowed her head in outward submission, her clenched fists hidden in the folds of her clothes. Fifteen years old, bound to this man, her wishes mattered naught.

A Note from
THE EDITORS

We hope you enjoyed another exciting volume in the Extraordinary Women of the Bible series, published by Guideposts. For over seventy-five years, Guideposts, a non-profit organization, has been driven by a vision of a world filled with hope. We aspire to be the voice of a trusted friend, a friend who makes you feel more hopeful and connected.

By making a purchase from Guideposts, you join our community in touching millions of lives, inspiring them to believe that all things are possible through faith, hope, and prayer. Your continued support allows us to provide uplifting resources to those in need. Whether through our communities, websites, apps, or publications, we inspire our audiences, bring them together, and comfort, uplift, entertain, and guide them. Visit us at guideposts.org to learn more.

We would love to hear from you. Write us at Guideposts, P.O. Box 5815, Harlan, Iowa 51593 or call us at (800) 932-2145. Did you love *At His Feet: Mary Magdalene's Story*? Leave a review for this product on guideposts.org/shop. Your feedback helps others in our community find relevant products.

Find inspiration, find faith, find Guideposts.

Shop our best sellers and favorites at
guideposts.org/shop

Or scan the QR code to go directly
to our Shop

Find more inspiring stories in these best-loved Guideposts fiction series!

Mysteries of Lancaster County

Follow the Classen sisters as they unravel clues and uncover hidden secrets in Mysteries of Lancaster County. As you get to know these women and their friends, you'll see how God brings each of them together for a fresh start in life.

Secrets of Wayfarers Inn

Retired schoolteachers find themselves owners of an old warehouse-turned-inn that is filled with hidden passages, buried secrets, and stunning surprises that will set them on a course to puzzling mysteries from the Underground Railroad.

Tearoom Mysteries Series

Mix one stately Victorian home, a charming lakeside town in Maine, and two adventurous cousins with a passion for tea and hospitality. Add a large scoop of intriguing mystery, and sprinkle generously with faith, family, and friends, and you have the recipe for *Tearoom Mysteries*.

Ordinary Women of the Bible

Richly imagined stories—based on facts from the Bible—have all the plot twists and suspense of a great mystery, while bringing you fascinating insights on what it was like to be a woman living in the ancient world.

To learn more about these books, visit Guideposts.org/Shop

Printed in the United States
by Baker & Taylor Publisher Services